# Too Many Notches

When ramrod Chev Best was shot dead on Hightower Ranch that day it sent a clear signal to the range boss Lawson Hannibal: he must fight fire with fire.

Hiring the services of gunfighters Chett Allison and the lethal Traven seemed the only way to defend the spread of terror and rid the rancher of his enemies no matter what the cost. But that cost was destined to prove far greater than anyone had feared.

And before the war was over, many would pay the highest price of all.

# Too Many Notches

## Chad Hammer

A Black Horse Western

ROBERT HALE · LONDON

ISBN 0 7090 7591 X

Robert Hale Limited
Clerkenwell House
Clerkenwell Green
London EC1R 0HT

Typeset by
Derek Doyle & Associates, Liverpool.
Printed and bound in Great Britain by
Antony Rowe Limited, Wiltshire.

# CHAPTER 1

# SEND FOR THE SHOOTER

Ramrod Chev Best looked nothing like a man who would soon be dead.

Spurring his buckskin along the fresh tracks leading up from the shotgun cabin he'd thrown up at remote Achilles Flats, and heading for Tramp Hill, he looked exactly the way the top hand on Hightower Ranch might be expected to look after awakening in the sickly grey of the false dawn to find his wayward milch cow had 'strayed' again, only to realize quickly as soon as he was in the saddle that the animal had been assisted in its break for freedom.

Stolen.

He now followed one set of cow tracks with the neat prints of a lightweight cow pony alongside.

Best's frown cut deep.

Trouble of just about every kind was no stranger to

sprawling Hightower these days. But what breed of crack-brained cow thief would risk his neck to ride alone into the very heartland of the heavily guarded spread to reach the hilly quarter section which Lawson Hannibal had recently turned over to his ramrod, then run off just a single, sway-backed milch cow?

Best was as practical as a branding-iron and this sort of behaviour had him both baffled and mad by the time he topped out on the sparsely treed crest, where he reined in with a fresh curse.

At his feet, more sign. The thief's horse had been tied up here to a pine for some considerable time while the lightweight rider had plainly paced to and fro smoking his way through several cigarettes before screwing up the nerve to go down after the cow. Jaw muscles working as he kicked away along the trace, Best slid his Fifty-Ninety-Five Express from scabbard and fingered a big cartridge into the chamber. Rustling was a killing offence in Vulcan County – as any blind fool should know. The tracks led him across the old Gilbert Trail and a half mile further on dipped downslope into a tightly wooded valley. No birds sang and the first rays of the sun were raising mist from the damp earth. The sign was sparse here yet he had little trouble following it down and across into a canyon rimmed with sycamore and dwarf pine.

A swift stutter of hoofbeats from up-canyon saw him jerk to a halt and whip up the heavy rifle.

Nothing to be seen; soon nothing to be heard.

The rider's frown cut deep as his glance swept the familiar terrain. The rustler's tracks angled away westward up-canyon. This canyon led to thorny scrub country studded with rocky spurs and gulches. Only a fool would tackle that kind of country for any reason; a double fool if encumbered by a milch cow.

Best massaged the back of his neck and felt the hair prickle against his fingers. Nothing about this thing felt right. But what option did a man have but to keep on?

A light pressure of the knees got the buckskin going again and hoof echoes piled around him as he covered maybe a half mile to the canyon mouth, where the going was soft and silent.

He reined in up where Tumbleweed Ridge reared above, and the quiet was graveyard deep.

In that moment, as his eyes swept the lifeless, sunwashed surrounds – the motionless trees and brooding outcroppings of gaunt stone – Chev Best suddenly knew, not merely sensed, that he should not be here. Should not have elected to follow the sign alone; should have instead raised the alarm then waited for his boys to arrive at the Flats.

The sound of the shot came shatteringly loud and a bullet slammed into the buckskin's withers as the rider threw himself headlong from the saddle.

There was cover close by but Best never reached it. In an instant the roar of the single shot gave way to a volley of murderous fire, and he saw through the gunsmoke the ghostly shapes of riders with rifles emerging from cover to form a circle of steel around him.

Then he was hit. Not just once; there was no telling how often as he spilled sideways, the lethal

Fifty-Ninety-Five slipping from his hands unfired, the world filled with insane noise as his senses began to desert him.

In his last moments of life he knew he'd been lured from the Flats to be murdered, knew who had killed him. Knew that at this moment, in this bloody place, the range war that had been threatening to rip Vulcan County apart for so long, had finally erupted.

Then nothing.

Heavy weather threatened: on the horizon a ridge of thunderheads churned and billowed and a spasm of wind seized a grove of distant pines, rippling shapes across its surface like massive fingers. The feeble autumn sun hung low to the west of Hightower Ranch headquarters and tired work horses in the yards mirrored the watery light in their eyes. Horned larks and longspurs heralded the sundown, their wild plaintive notes coming from no apparent direction.

'Would you care for some coffee, Miss Angelina?'

'No thank you, Betsy.'

'Could need it for your strength.'

'Betsy!'

'All right, Missy, all right, I'm a-going.'

The door closed on the maid's back and Angelina Hannibal remained seated at the piano keyboard in the wide parlor of the ranch house, picking out muted chords, her head to one side as she listened to the murmuring noises of the great house and the muted sounds of activity from outside.

Soon she would be obliged to present herself in the dining-room for supper, but for the present she was enjoying the calm of the moment following recent catastrophic events. It seemed to the rancher's daughter that Hightower had known little but troubles and upheavals in recent months, and of course all hint of normality had gone out the window ten days earlier with the murder of Chev Best.

'Angelina!'

It was her father's voice, coming from the study that flanked the living-room. The girl's eighteen-year-old face pouted prettily as she lifted her fingers from the keys and sat silently. Perhaps he would think she had left the room, gone to another part of the house where she couldn't hear him calling.

'Miss!'

There was no mistaking that tone. That was his cattle baron's voice and all Hightower was familiar with it. She closed the lid and rose. 'Yes, Father, what is it?'

'I don't propose to shout across the whole house to you, young lady. You will be so good as to join me in my study.'

Although feeling guilty over how she felt, Angelina rose and went quickly through to the book-lined room, forcing a smile as she entered.

The rancher didn't look up. He was seated at his desk, a heavy-set greying man in his middle fifties whose face was powerful and commanding, but ashen today and lined with concern. The desk lamp had been lighted, for the brooding gloom of the oncoming storm had already penetrated the house.

The girl felt a small tug at her heart as she studied the furrowed brow, the creased cheeks. Worry had worn the cattle king down in recent times, yet his handwriting was firm as he tallied up the rows of figures before him. In addition, today he wore a black crêpe armband in tribute to his murdered foreman, the one man he'd always said he couldn't do without. He glanced up with a smile.

'You look very charming this evening, Daughter.'

'Thank you, Father. Was there something you wanted?'

'Indeed there is.' He indicated the sheets before him. 'I'm attempting to complete this work before dinner, but the men are making such a racket out front I'm being distracted. You must have noticed?'

She hadn't. Now she did. A frown creased her brows. She identified the harsh, growly tones of Buck Taller and the responding twang of Hogue Kells. What on earth were they so excited about?

'I'll tell them to be quiet,' she said, moving to the door.

'Ask – I think that would be preferable, my dear. Civility costs nothing, remember?'

The girl bit her lower lip. She was strong-willed and opinionated in a way her father found admirable and supportive most times. But sometimes she could offend, especially in her dealings with certain recent new recruits of whom she strongly disapproved.

Buck Taller and Hogue Kells topped that list at the moment. The pair were neither cowhands, herders or nighthawks, but rather gunmen hired specifically to bolster security in Hightower's ever-deepening conflict with the neighbouring Cross-T.

'It wouldn't be any effort to be civil to them if they

were anything like gentlemen,' she retorted. 'It's all I can do to speak to that awful Taller – and Kells is little better. I wish . . . I wish . . .'

'Now, Angie, we've been over all this before. There's nothing we can do about it. You understand as well as I the necessity of such men being here, considering the ever-worsening situation with Cross-T. If only the authorities were more involved we wouldn't have to take such extreme measures to protect ourselves, and after what happened to Chev . . .'

His voice trailed off. Ramrod Best had been the most popular man on the spread. Even Angelina had liked him, and she could be a difficult person to please.

'Whatever you say, Father.'

'There's the girl. Just tell them to tone it down and move off from the porch, will you?'

'Gunmen!' she muttered under her breath as she went down the long carpeted hallway. How she despised the breed! Arrogant inhuman brutes, they were without a single saving grace from her point of view. She often wondered if trying to save Hightower from the depredations of the voracious Stobaughs could be worth such extreme measures; she saw it as lowering themselves to the same level as the enemy they despised.

And now, in an action which she saw as quite simply adding fuel to the fire, her father had seen fit to make arrangements to add further to their considerable gun strength in the wake of Best's murder by hiring yet another gunhand, a 'renowned professional' as he'd described this murderous brute, whoever he might be.

Where would it all end?

Pausing now at the opened double cedar doors which gave out on to the front porch, she told herself she might simply have to go stay with her relatives in Carson City until the troubles were over, as her father had so often suggested.

She could cope with drought, heat, dust, falling cattle prices and rough-mannered cowboys but there was a limit to a person's tolerance. And for her this came in the shape of the two men she now singled out with a scowling glare. She believed she might have left the place the day her father hired Taller and Kells, but for the fact that the Carson City branch of the Hannibal clan were stuffy and tedious beyond belief. As she moved towards the noisy group she realized their boisterous excitement seemed to be directed to something beyond the ranch yard. One of the gunmen was pointing eastward while his companions continued arguing. Following Buck Taller's gesture, Angelina realized there was a horse-man coming down the town trail, riding swiftly with his hat pushed back, kicking up a plume of yellow dust that contrasted sharply with the deepening purple of the storm clouds to his rear.

'Gotta be him, boys!' Taller said loudly.

'How do you know?' countered rangy Kells, hands resting on his gun handles.

'How the hell do you think? Take another look and tell me what this is if that ain't some breed of hardcase, mister.'

12

'Hi there, Miss Angela,' greeted Taller. 'Your hotshot new gunfighter's showed up at last by the looks.' The man's grin was malicious. 'Whooewee! If you don't like the cut of me and Kells' jib none, you're gonna hate this one, I'm thinking. I could smell trouble coming off him as soon as he showed over the rise.'

The horseman was within a hundred yards of the title gate now. Angelina saw that he was a big man, bigger even than Taller, who was well over six feet tall. He carried himself very straight in the saddle and, even at distance, she was aware of the arrogance of his carriage. His hair was overlong and a strange light sheened from a powerful, sardonic face.

And of course, around lean flat hips were buckled a pair of big ugly revolvers nestled deep and snug in cutaway holsters.

Pale now, she swung her back and retreated to the study. The rancher was still at his desk, chewing his quill and fingering his arm band – probably brooding about the dead ramrod again if she was any judge.

'There's someone coming in, Father. The men seem to think it's the man you're expecting. What was his name again? Machiavelli? Diablo. . . ?'

Ignoring her sarcasm, Hannibal rose and inserted his hard-nibbed pen in a kern holder. 'Distinguished type, so I'm informed. That fit his description, honey?'

'He looks about as distinguished as a naked redskin in war paint with a scalping knife in either hand and—'

'Come on,' the rancher said, forcing a smile as he

13

slipped his hand around her waist. 'You're just biased. Let's take a look at your catch.'

Sometimes Angelina still enjoyed being treated as a child; it made her feel small and protected. Other times she chafed at this habit of her father's so fiercely that even Aunt Hortense, Uncle Cyril and her poisonous cousins Clarabell and Elma Hannibal from Carson City seemed an almost attractive alternative to life on Hightower.

The couple quit the room together and went through to the porch just as the rider came across the yard astride his beautiful horse and reined in before the group lounging on the wide steps.

Angelina realized the stranger was even bigger than he'd appeared at a distance. Seated astride the midnight black horse that bore the marks of long hard travel, he loomed up in the fading light, big-shouldered, slim-hipped, thick-armed. He wore a checkered wool shirt and faded Levi's, and his twin Colts hung from a broad leather belt ornamented by a huge steel buckle.

But it was the face that drew the eye. There was something savage and sardonic in the arrangement of the features, something distinctly piratical about the black arch of the brows, the hooded, almost sleeping looking eyes.

Although sitting motionless now, there was still about him an air of explosive energy, of power almost too great to be contained in one body.

To Angelina Hannibal, the stranger was the most frightening man she'd ever seen, as his appraising stare slid away from her and drilled hard at her father.

'You Hannibal?'

'I am Colonel Hannibal, sir.'

This seemed to amuse the man, who smiled broadly, displaying teeth that looked powerful enough to crush bone. 'Howdy do, Hannibal.'

The cattleman flushed, yet his voice remained even as he said, 'You are Chett Allison, I take it?'

The man gave no sign he had heard. Instead he swung his hooded gaze back to Angelina. She felt his eyes go over her in a more blatant way than she had ever experienced. She forced herself to remain cool and poised, and after another enigmatic grin the man directed his attention to the ranch gunmen who were grouped together, watching him warily.

He sneered.

'So, I take it you are the two-gun heroes who can't handle a clutch of grubstake rustlers, huh?'

The Hightower riders bristled at the insult, some fingering their gun handles as they glanced at Taller and Kells to see their reaction. They waited for Taller to speak up, their eyes glittering yellow in the dusky gloom. Hannibal's decision to import a big-name gunfighter at great expense in the aftermath of the Best killing was viewed by the hardcases as an implied reflection on them all. They knew Taller was sore about the Allison affair and were expecting sparks to fly.

Buck Taller took his time in sizing up the newcomer, then appraised his own backing before speaking up in his familiar whiskey growl.

'We've heard plenty about you, Allison. Too much, a man might say. We'd like to tell you how plum excited we are to have a shooter of your calibre show up here in the boondocks to teach us poorboy guntippers how to suck eggs, but I guess that'll have to wait. You see, here on Hightower, it's what a man can do, not what he claims he can, that cuts the ice. We'll be working together here and if you want to get along with us we—'

'Who says I want to?' the newcomer interrupted. 'And as for working with losers, forget it. I work with my pard and we don't need nobody else, never did and never will. So, seeing as we understand one another now, why don't you boys just run along and get back to your knitting. I got business with Hannibal here.'

It was suddenly very quiet on Hightower Ranch. Taller's heavy jaw had slipped loose as he glanced uncertainly from the newcomer to Hannibal and back. This was a rare position for the top gunhand to find himself in. He'd come to the spread with a repu-tation which he'd built on impressively since with fists, guns and a bull-headed brand of raw courage. But what he was facing here was something new. Taller was fast, tough and had good backing, yet he felt neither angry nor confident enough to move his hand any closer to the butt of his .45 than it was now, as long as those mocking eyes continued to bore into him.

He was waiting for the boss man to save the moment – but the newcomer acted first. The black horse was suddenly kneed forward, a big boot swung loose from a stirrup and caught Taller in the chest, forcing him to take two stumbling steps backwards.

'Didn't you hear me, pilgrim? I told you to haul freight.'

'Oh, Father!' Angelina gasped with a sharp intake of breath, seeing Taller's face flush with fury.

Hannibal was already moving. Stepping quickly between his men and the horseman, he spoke sharply and with natural authority. 'There is no call for this kind of behaviour, mister. I invited you down here to fight, but not with my own men. You will forthwith kindly keep your tongue and your boots to yourself.'

He backed up his words with a stern glare salvaged from his Civil War days as a cavalry officer. The big rider just shrugged and smiled carelessly as the rancher turned to Taller. 'Supper's fixed down at the cookhouse, Buck. You and the boys best get along there. I'll handle this.'

'Whatever you say, boss man.' Taller was regaining some of his composure now the danger of the moment seemed to be passing. 'But you make sure you wise him up about just who we are, and how we none of us aim to take none of his cheap jaw.'

'Supper, mister!' Hannibal snapped.

With a final scowl, Buck Taller spun on his heel and strode off into the darkness, Kells and the bunch dutifully following. The horseman chuckled loudly but Hannibal interrupted him angrily.

'There was no call for any of that, mister. I'm beginning to wonder if I was ill-advised in offering you a contract.'

'Hell, man, nobody where I hail from gives a toss how a feller treats small-time backshooters.'

'And pray, what are you, sir?' It was Angelina, now standing in the light streaming from the doorway. 'A big-time backshooter, I presume? And, of course, that makes all the difference.'

'Big-time, yes, Miss. Backshooter – nope.'

Strangely enough the man didn't appear annoyed by her attack. He went on in an even tone, addressing her directly. 'You see, Miss, whenever a feller like me shows at a new stand, he's just got to show the hired help where they stand from the get-go. Small-time gunslicks can get mighty biggety at times after they ride roughshod over a couple of nesters, or drunken breeds packing single-shot cavalry pistols. And if you let them sass you and get away with it, why, next thing you know they'll be wanting to roughshod you. They figure if you talk soft you are soft.' He shrugged and spread two big hands. 'My bossy ways can save a lot of messy shooting in the long run.'

Angelina's face was unreadable. But inside she could feel her hostility waver a little. She had to admit the stranger was not without a certain virile charm, and she suspected that what he said made sense. She'd enjoyed watching Taller being given short shrift, but allowed none of these feelings to show when she replied, 'They might have killed you, Mister Allison. How do you know Taller, or any of them, might not be your better with a gun?'

'Nobody is, that's why.' The response came out flat and emphatic as the newcomer swung down from his saddle. He mounted the porch to stand between father and daughter, a towering figure with barn-door shoulders, hands on narrow hips. 'Another

18

thing while I'm at it. I ain't Chett Allison.'

Both stared uncomprehendingly. Hannibal found his tongue first. 'You're not Allison? But we've been expecting him at any time. How—?'

'Oh, he's coming along right enough. But I came on ahead, sorta to check out the lie of the land, if you know what I mean. I'm Traven.'

Angelina felt a chill run down her spine. Along with Chett Allison, Traven had also been a dangerous name in Nevada for a number of years. The papers they received intermittently from Carson City carried reports on the pair from time to time, stories of bloody gun battles, dead men and weeping widows. For some reason, the press seemed of the view that Allison in particular was some kind of gun hero, although this might be attributable to his reputed impressive appearance and style more so than what he did with his guns. But the press had painted this second man well, she realized. She'd never heard the term 'hero' applied to Ned Traven. But they did say he was a dangerous man, which she could readily believe.

She watched as her father nodded and extended his hand, a gentleman in all circumstances.

'I'm pleased you are here, Mr Traven, even though I'm not at all sure I can afford both of you if your fees are anything near as criminally high as Allison's—'

'Did I say anything about money?' Traven challenged as he swallowed the rancher's hand in his own big paw. He indicated Angelina. 'Your daughter?'

Hannibal nodded and performed the introductions.

'Mister Traven,' she said formally.

'Howdy, bright-eyes.'

Hannibal reacted angrily. 'Now see here, fellow, you will kindly treat my daughter with respect or by heaven—'

'Ah, don't get your tail in a crack, man.' Traven shrugged. 'I ain't no skirt-chaser, just trying to be friendly.' He stretched hugely, yawned loudly. 'Where do I sleep?'

The man's abrupt shift of moods was something they would have to grow accustomed to, so it would seem. Hannibal continued to eye the man uneasily and with some suspicion, but Angelina sounded surprisingly casual as she said, 'There is accommodation available for both you and Mister Allison in either the house or out with the men, whichever you would prefer.'

'Well, thank you for that, bright-eyes. You know, there are some places they expect a man to sleep with the horses – like he was a common hand or something. Others want you to take their best beds on account they're scared if they don't play up to us we might start in shooting them up at the supper table, just out of natural cussedness.' He winked. 'Show me my room, gal.'

He turned quickly and commenced to unstrap his warbag. 'Hannibal, see to it that somebody takes good care of my horse, will you? He's my good pard, and it might be an idea to let 'em know that at the stables, if you get my meaning?'

Hannibal nodded and frowned. 'Must you retire immediately? We have business to discuss and—'

'What's to discuss?' Traven replied, offloading his roll from the horse and slinging it over one shoulder. 'You wired Chett and told him you had troubles. He wired back and you OK'd his price – and here I am.'

'But surely you want to know the details of what's been going on here, why I was forced to take these extreme measures?'

'It'll all still be going on tomorrow, won't it? Anyways, Chett'll be here himself come morning, he's the one that handles all the details.'

'Well, I suppose if you must retire, then you must. Angel, will you. . . ?'

'Of course, Father. This way, Mr Traven.'

Surprised by her seeming lack of unease in the big man's presence now, Angelina led the way for the sleeping quarters in the east wing. The sprawling mansion had been added to over the years, modern in some sections, old in others. The way took them through gypsum-coated passages where wall-brack-eted lamps burned softly and on past a doorway to the scullery where a curious maid peered out, her eyes popping when she saw 'Miz Angel' walking by trailed by a giant stranger who gave her a leering grin and scared her half to death.

Angelina finally halted before two doors which faced each other across the width of a short corridor which gave on to a small balcony overlooking the yard and horse corrals. 'These are our guest rooms, Mr Traven. You can choose whichever one you prefer.'

He leaned the point of a shoulder against the door casement and arched wicked eyebrows, the lamplight softening the deep indentation of the knife scar and the hard planes and brutal angles of his face.

'Hell, either one'll suit me. And thank you kindly, bright-eyes.'

She was less annoyed by his familiarity than she'd been at first. But she was still smarting over the way the man spoke to her father and said as much.

'Mister Traven, as you and Mister Allison may be working and living here for some time, I must ask you to show some more respect when addressing my father. I think the least you can do is address him as "Colonel".'

'Colonel, huh? Is that a genuine rank or just some cotton-picking honorary you can buy off any notary public if you've got the dinero?'

'My father rose to that rank in the Confederacy during the War between the States, I'll have you know.'

'Most folks I know from hereabouts that went through the War ended up broke by the time they returned home. Reckon your daddy came out of it better than most. Ah well, not much use of a war unless someone makes something out of it, so I always say.'

She felt herself colouring.

'Father slaved to rebuild the ranch, took risks and fought with all he had to succeed. But I'm sure such things would not impress someone like yourself who believes the only way to acquire things is to terrorize and kill for them.'

'Bright-eyes, it might amaze you to know just how few things impress me any which way.'

'I doubt that, Mr Traven. I'm sure virtually every-thing I learned about a man like yourself would either amaze or disgust me. Good-night.'

'Now hold on hard there,' he said, moving to block her path by resting one big hand against the wall. 'You sure are a tetchy filly, ain't you.' He dropped his arm. 'OK, OK, don't get sore. I'll make a deal. I'll treat old Daddy Big Bucks right if that'll make your little heart happy. On one condition.'

'Which is?'

'That you call me Trav.'

Her eyes narrowed. 'Why should you want me to do that?'

'A man don't have to have a reason for everything. So, what do you say?'

Angelina hesitated a moment. Then she shrugged. 'Very well . . . Trav.' He dropped his arm and she took two steps along the passageway, then paused. 'One more question. . . ?'

'Sorry, I'm getting tired and bored. You'll have to find out for yourself.'

'Find out what?'

'Honey, you're as easy to see through as the mica windows on a mint-new buggy. I'm just Chett's side-kick, but seeing as I scare the hell out of you, you're sweating at the thought of what he might turn out to be like – two heads, or dangling fresh-cut scalps off his shell belt maybe. Well, I'm sorry all to hell but you're just going to have to wait and see for your-self.'

He jerked the door to his room open, hurled his roll inside. 'Only thing I'll tell you is you're due for a surprise – one hell of a surprise if you want to know the truth.'

Angelina stood motionless in the hallway after the door crashed shut, listening to him chuckling and repeating the words, '. . . one hell of a surprise.'

Slowly she turned away and followed the passage-way leading to the front. A glance into the dining-room as she passed, showed that the servants had already laid out the great table for a meal. The flow-ers weren't exactly as she'd instructed but she could-n't be concerned with such things. Not now.

On the empty porch it was quiet and cold, her breath forming thin gusts of fog in the darkness. She thought of the gunman's arrival. Then she thought about all the other troubles on Hightower and the murder of good Chev Best, and there seemed only one thing for it.

Slipping through to the parlour, she went to the liquor cabinet and poured herself a stiff shot. She felt sinful, drinking hard liquor at this time. But every instinct warned this would be no normal kind of day. Maybe normal days on Hightower belonged to the past now, as did so many other things she had once held high.

After Chev Best, a war was inevitable. She thought about the man who was to appear the following day.

She thought she'd seen the worst of men warped by brutality and gun pride in men like Buck Taller and Hogue Kells. But the arrogant Traven was a more frightening and dangerous proposition than she could have imagined, yet he was only Allison's 'sidekick', as the gunfighter had said. If such an arrogant and intimidating man would seem happy with that subservient role, what sort of monster must the master be? Back on the porch, time slipped by unnoticed until the plump housemaid appeared in the double doors to inform that supper was ready.

'Thank you, Maria.'

She allowed her gaze to play over the ranch a final time before re-entering the house. Light rain was falling now, the flash of lightning and the guttural thunder voices to the north warned of rougher weather on the way. It was a night of foreboding, of menace that had no shape or substance, yet tautened the nerves to agonised awareness. Life on Hightower had been anything but peaceful or pleasant in recent months, but instinct warned that with Allison's coming, it would all become a thousand times worse. With a shudder that was only partly caused by the chill, Angelina went inside and closed the door behind her.

# CHAPTER 2

# TWO OF A KIND

In a way it was a kind of a game the gunfighter played without always being conscious of it. He called the game Travelling Incognito. If played successfully it enabled him to travel from one place to another, showing up someplace here, or leaving another there, without being recognized, identified or singled out for undue attention.

It got tougher to succeed at the Game each year as his notoriety grew. Yet he continued to play, partly because of the challenge involved, but primarily in order that he might enjoy a little privacy and anonymity during those rare periods between jobs when he was not in the full glare of the spotlight and grabbing the headlines.

He'd succeeded up until now over the past night and into the morning while riding the high iron down from Comstock Wells to Buffalo Gate. He'd secured the very back seat in Car Four where, muffled up in a belted leather raincoat with the winged collars turned high and his flat brimmed hat tilted low over his face, he was just another lone traveller heading south, not bothering anybody or being bothered as he ate up the dark miles to his destination, which was reached dead on schedule, 9 a.m. sharp.

He'd never been to Buffalo Gate but from what could be seen through rain-streaked windows it was all too familiar; lofted falsefronts, acres of churned-up mud surrounding the depot buildings, street lights still burning late like the intention was to try and replace the sunshine not seen now in over a week.

His mind must have been on other things as he rose and took down his satchel – most likely the job ahead. Whatever the case, as he moved to the aisle, the conductor emerged from the box car, politely paused and motioned for him to go ahead.

'After you,' the gunfighter said.

'No, sir, I insist.'

The gunfighter shook his head slowly. 'Don't walk behind me.'

He spoke softly but it seemed all in that noisy car heard, for every head turned as the conductor flushed, muttered, 'Sorry, sir,' then hurried on by.

The gunfighter frowned and the faces looked away. But they had seen what they had seen, and most understood. Men of his profession hated to have anyone behind them, anytime, anyplace. And by the time he'd followed them out on to the platform, where they stopped to stare covertly, he could tell they had him tabbed. Rugged up in his big leather coat and turned down hat, they realized he had the look, a look that Buffalo Gate and Vulcan County had become all too familiar with over recent weeks and months as the range war flared, and strangers with guns began walking their streets.

He shrugged and went back to the horse car, no longer caring. It was, after all, only the Game. Reality was replacing it now. With the train journey behind him he was now just two hours' ride short of his ultimate destination.

The platform was clearing rapidly as the gunfighter moved across the planks of the platform to the covered, open-sided end of the depot building. A stage was drawing away, the poncho-garbed driver hunched over his reins on the seat up top. A wide street angled away northwards from the depot, reflected light from glass windows mirroring in the puddles of rain water.

The conductor had preceded him to the horse box. The ramp was already down and a surly man in a shabby uniform was leading his horse down. The animal whiskered a greeting and the gunfighter reached up to pat its ugly roman nose. Conductor and attendant watched him nervously as he took the reins, looped them over the grulla's head, then lashed his satchel to the saddle.

Then, 'Going far, mister?' The conductor's curiosity outrode his nervousness.

He flipped the man a coin and swung up, coat tails flapping in the chill wind. He guided the horse down the platform ramp then rode the length of the nearest street before crossing over the river bridge. There he cut sharply south and had Hightower Ranch between his horse's ears.

Angelina Hannibal waited until her father finished picking his way through breakfast before setting her coffee cup down in front of her with an air of finality.

'We simply must try the capital one more time, father.'

The rancher came out of his moody introspection with a grunt. 'Pardon?'

'You heard perfectly well. The state troopers – they're the only ones who can stop this madness.'

She paused to gesture towards the rear of the house.

'That – that person – here in our house. It's an outrage. So arrogant and offensive, and so plainly eager to begin killing people. He's a monster. So we can only imagine what sort of bloody-handed creature Allison must be. It's just not right, Father. We shouldn't have to traffic with such people simply in order to protect what is ours. You've got to send them packing; there's got be another way.'

'If there was another way, don't you think I'd have taken it, girl? This decision has kept me awake night after night, Angie, believe me it has. Good Lord! It was bad enough when I was forced to import Taller and Kells to give our defences some teeth. But now . . .'

'At least they are workers as well as gunmen.'

'They are not gunmen capable of preventing killers from invading the heart of the range and

29

murdering our finest man, my daughter.'

'There has to be another way. The troopers—'

'Can and will do nothing,' Hannibal cut in. 'You recall when I personally visited State HQ six weeks ago, pleading for assistance? They as much as told me straight that petty quarrels between cattlemen over stock and boundaries must be settled privately, that the Government had much more to concern itself than trivial disturbances.'

'The Vulcan County war has never been trivial – much less than ever now.'

This was true.

On a raw frontier accustomed to violent conflicts stemming from unfenced range, cattle ownership, water-rights and plain old-fashioned greed, the conflict between Hightower and Cross-T ranches had attained its own gory eminence over time. Dating back several years to the time when Jared Stobaugh and Lawson Hannibal had taken up huge adjoining tracts of cattle country south of the county capital, the feuding rivalry had erupted early and had grown in viciousness and scope ever since.

If there was a single ignition point for the conflict, it lay in the simple fact that the former southern gentleman, Hannibal, was by nature horrified to find himself neighbour to a man like Stobaugh, who had survived the war to boast about the small Mississippi town which a company of bluecoats under his command had razed to the ground.

But even this was not enough to have triggered off the full-scale hostility which lay between them now. Gold was the trigger. For there was gold here in

Nevada Territory – gold-on-the-hoof to meet the needs of a meat-hungry East. Both men wanted his share of that wealth, and more. And both being astute and experienced cattlemen, they flourished and grew stronger while lesser ranchers folded and moved on.

Friction also flourished.

With two ever increasing herds roaming largely unfenced range, with cowhands of both spreads meeting and contesting the ownership of unbranded stock, fences being erected and torn down by the enemy on a regular basis, the outcome was inevitable. Arguments led to fights, threats – and eventually gunplay.

In one such explosion involving guns, Hannibal's only son lost his life, the single incident changing a rangeland feud into open war.

It was directly following this tragedy that Hannibal hired five professional gunmen cum cowhands, the Buck Taller bunch, to protect his life and property.

Jared Stobaugh lost several hands in various bloody skirmishes against this new element introduced into the conflict, before realizing what he must do to counter the enemy's new strength. Overnight, the Cross-T's ranks were swollen by the addition of Seneca McVey, Drum Cormorant and Judd Smith – gunslingers all.

The bellow of cattle and the moan of the prairie winds were now intermingled with a new sound that had become depressingly familiar, the crash of sixgun and rifle. As a result, the Vulcan County War became a topic for debate, interest and condemnation throughout the territory. Yet there was still no sign of genuine interest or assistance of any tangible kind by the government.

That had been six months ago and the war had been stepping up in fury ever since. Elections were held in the capital and delegations from the new state government visited the troubled region. But so confused were the records and grants of ownership that the best they could recommend was that the warring parties simply get together, bury their enmities and come up with workable solutions before they lost everything.

Then they were gone, returning to the comparative calm and safety of their plush new appointments in the capital.

A peaceful solution may have been attainable even at this late stage had not Jared Stobaugh died from wounds received in a clash with Hightower, leaving his elder son, Wolf, at the helm of Cross-T.

The well-named Wolf was brutal and elemental, and many, including Colonel Hannibal, anticipated that the man's own nature must surely bring him down. This had not happened. Instead, Cross-T affairs ran smoothly while the ranch force grew in strength. There had to be a reason for this, or so the county pundits reasoned, and so was born the theory which had gained strength and credence over time.

Plainly there was additional money and a keen intelligence masterminding Cross-T's continuing expansion and power in the land.

Wolf Stobaugh gambled money faster than he could get his hands on it. And although ruthless and intimidating, nobody had ever accused old Jared's son and heir of being too smart.

Thus the theory: someone or some organization must have been recruited to mastermind and finance Cross-T's slow and steady surge upwards.

But who?

This was still a question that preoccupied drinkers at Buffalo Gate's long bars and the porch rockers sages, while a canny few believed they already had the part answer in the shape of persistent rumour that a thus far unnamed shadowy government official, a wheeler-dealer and alleged dabbler in matters far removed from his official duties, was in fact the new and potent driving force behind the Cross-T's determination to become the power above all in Vulcan County. A mystery man of alleged high ambitions with brains, acumen and a talent for tactics.

Whether this theory was rooted in truth or not, none could be sure. Yet tactics in the range war had altered significantly and alarmingly just two weeks ago when Chev Best died under a hail of hot lead.

Best had been the most popular man on the spread, tough, honest and likeable, and a fighter through and through. Even so, it was less the loss of such a man than the manner in which he'd died that set the tinder to the flame. Men on both sides of the war had died before, in rustling raids, gun duels, revenge missions. In a range war, such deaths almost rated as 'natural causes'. The Hightower ramrod's case was very different. An enemy force had infiltrated Hightower, had lain in wait for Best to show then cut him down from ambush – a cold-blooded and premeditated assassination.

The following day the colonel had written to a certain influential contact in Carson City in the hope of securing assistance of a professional kind. He was prepared to pay out whatever was the going price for a top-range gunfighter and peacekeeper of the highest calibre.

Nothing could convince him that this was not the right course of action, not even his daughter's, at times, eloquent arguments.

She was arguing now but Hannibal was having difficulty in understanding her words. With good reason. Someone with leather lungs had started hooting and hollering over by the yard gate, and heads were popping from windows to see what the fuss was about.

'Damnation!' Hannibal snapped, rising from his chair. 'What now? Who the devil is that? Can't a man find any peace, even for a moment?'

The girl moved swiftly to the window and looked out. She stiffened in surprise, and when she failed to speak, her father joined her.

It was a grey overcast morning with blown leaves skittering across the ranchyard. Directly out from the breakfast-room windows, Traven stood in the cold wind with his shirt unbuttoned to the waist, bareheaded and laughing. Suddenly he lunged forward as a rider rounded the cookshack corner and swung down from an ugly-looking grulla stallion.

The men grasped hands and Traven's booming voice carried to every corner of the wind-blowing yard. 'Howdy, pard. Right on time, b'God – as usual. Good to see you, man, good to see you.'

The Hannibals stared at one another for a long moment in complete silence. When they looked out again, the newcomer was shedding a grimed weather coat to reveal a stylish broadcloth suit, string tie – and guns. Twin sixguns thonged low on the thighs, gunfighter-style.

'That ... that's Chett Allison?' Hannibal said wonderingly.

'Impossible,' Angelina retorted. 'Killers simply don't look like that. And I should know, being surrounded by the breed day and night without—'

'C'mon, you horse-faced buzzard!' Traven's voice drowned out the woman's. 'I told 'em you'd be starving by the time you got here. Let's go see what this cowboy-poisoning cook's got on the skillet. Funny thing here, but folks don't seem to realize that shooting up badasses and dodging lead hones a man's appetite something fierce. Let's hustle. The boys'll take care of old Leadbelly for you.'

Uncomprehendingly, father and daughter drew back from the windows as the two tall men moved towards the house. They heard the maid attend the door, then the approaching steps coming down the hallway. Not even aware of her actions, Angelina was straightening her skirt nervously and quickly patted her hair to assure neatness. The door crashed open and Traven came striding through.

'Folks, this here is Chett Allison!'

The man who stepped forward and bowed formally was of identical height to Traven. He

35

extended his right hand. 'Colonel Hannibal, a pleasure, sir.'

The voice was strong, well-modulated with the hint of a clipped midwestern accent. It wasn't the colonel's nature to stammer, but he did so then before recovering. 'Er, pleased to make your acquaintance – sir. My daughter. Angelina, meet Mr Allison.'

'Call me Chett,' Allison said.

The gunfighter turned to face Angelina, and she found herself looking into a pair of the most disarmingly direct grey eyes she'd ever seen. Again he gave that slight, formal inclination of his head and murmured, 'Miss Angelina. A pleasure.'

Ned Traven stood back with one hip outthrust, his brutal features reflecting cynical pleasure as he chuckled.

'Lordy, just look at these folks' faces, will you, pard? And you know why they don't know if they're coming or going? Me, of course!' He thumped his chest with a clenched fist. 'Me! I blew in, they took one look at me, decided I was the scariest thing they ever did see, and mistook me for you.' He chuckled as deep as his liver. 'Sure. I might've kinda conveyed the notion you might have been even uglier, meaner and more of a maverick than I ever knew how to be. Now they can't rightly believe you ain't got two heads and a forked tail. Guess the surprise is on you, folks.'

No matter what the Hannibals might have expected, Chett Allison would still have come as a total surprise. To cover his confusion, the colonel began barking orders to his servants, lined up against the rear wall, and they hurried off to fetch bacon, coffee and hotcakes while the housemaid took the newcomer's hat, Hannibal poured whiskeys from a decanter and Angelina feigned interest in what was happening outside to conceal her confused feelings.

She stole a quick glance over her shoulder. Even though both men were tall, she realized that Allison was lean, almost slight in comparison with Traven's muscular bulk. She couldn't deny he was strikingly handsome, with a calm, almost contemplative, manner that contrasted oddly with the other gunman's swaggering style. His face was fine-featured, clean-shaven and slightly pale. Her gaze dropped to the gun handles visible beneath his open jacket then back to his face. He was nodding to something her father was saying, yet seemed aloof, with a touch of arrogance.

The arrogance seemed to be the single feature he shared with Ned Traven.

The food arrived and they took their places around the long polished table, the tall frames of the hired guns seemingly too outsized for the carved period furniture, fine linen and gleaming silver service.

Recovered from his initial surprise by this, the colonel was soon looking relaxed as they politely discussed such matters as Allison's journey and the latest political news from Carson City.

Hannibal did most of the talking, sizing up his man with shrewd eyes. Allison replied slowly and thoughtfully to each question directed his way. Traven wolfed down enough bacon for six, his cynically amused expression in evidence throughout the meal. Angelina was silent, still fighting to reconcile herself to the fact that, even though Chett Allison was obviously a gentleman of some breeding and style, he was still nothing more or less than a hired gunfighter. A killer.

After his first sip of after-dinner coffee, when the dishes had been removed and brandy poured, Allison leaned back in his high-backed chair and looked directly at the colonel.

'I've been following the Vulcan County war in the northern press for some time, Colonel Hannibal. How bad is it, really? And who is most at fault?'

'It's about as bad as it can be, following the murder of my ramrod, sir,' Hannibal replied with equal directness. 'As for who is the aggressor, well, I don't see why that should be of any great significance. Suffice to say that you will be fighting Cross-T and their minions and—'

'A moment,' Allison interrupted. 'Let's make something quite clear. I never work for any party until I understand a given situation completely. I'm here, but I'm certainly not working for you yet.'

Hannibal was taken aback. Before he could respond, Angelina cut in sharply, 'Surely the fact that you have come so far should give us reason to believe you intend to work for us, Mr Allison?'

'Wrong, bright-eyes,' Traven drawled, puffing out a great cloud of pungent cigar smoke. 'You see, the man's got principles.' He made 'principles' sound like a complaint. 'He won't work until he's convinced he's doing the right thing. Me? I don't give one worn-out damn who I shoot or how many.'

'You've been out in the mesquite too long, Trav,' Allison said with a smile. 'We don't cuss before ladyfolks. Remember?' Sober again, he turned to Hannibal. 'My pard could have phrased it better, but he got the gist across. I want to know exactly what's going on here before I start choosing sides. And now we understand one another, let's start from the beginning.'

The cattle king stared wonderingly at his daughter for a moment. Then he slugged down a glass of sherry and finally began to talk.

By the time the discussion wound up an hour later, Hightower Ranch had the top gun it wanted, along with a second gun it hadn't really expected, but in the end decided it needed.

The colonel was weary but satisfied by the time the dealing was done. However, he found himself incapable of meeting the look in his daughter's eyes.

# CHAPTER 3

# TUMBLEWEED GUNS

Gunsmoke stung Buck Taller's eyes and set him cursing again.

The whole thing had been a carefully concocted trap designed to sucker them in like gullible yokels. This was now all too clear to the Hightower gunfighter as he lay sprawled behind cover, pinned down tight with Hogue Kells and three ranch riders under the raking fire flaring down at them from Tumbleweed Ridge above.

Filling their regular roles of riding guard with the working cowhands, the colonel's gunmen had come upon twenty head of prime unbranded stock in this shallow depression in the shadow of a range of rough cliffs and crags a short distance from Hightower's western border with the enemy Cross-T.

He should have suspected a trap; a foul-cursing

40

Taller realized that now.

For weeks the hands had been scouring this rough region for stock as part of the annual winter roundup. It had only been at the outset of the hunt that sizeable numbers of cattle been encountered and run back to the mustering yards. Shortly, with both ranches gathering at the same time, the man-shy beeves got spooked and were now mainly to be found alone or in skittish pairs. But today's searching party had been so elated to discover a full twenty head of prime stuff here, they'd swooped straight in from the timber line to scoop them when gun hell broke loose.

'I thought you were supposed to be keeping a sharp lookout while I covered the boys?' he spat at Kells, crunched down tight behind a deadfall close by.

Kells cussed.

'You're supposed to be the top gun, fella. Ain't top guns supposed to see everything, smell everything, know every goddamn thing?'

Taller shrugged off the sarcasm, suddenly, gloomily, reminding himself of the bitter fact that he was no longer top gun on Hightower Ranch. Overnight he'd plummeted to Number Three. And that was how he'd be remembered when he was dead, he figured, unless he came up with something damn smart here in a big hurry. Buck Taller – dead loser.

He cursed afresh as a fresh volley of fire chopped down. He struggled to worm his way deeper into the shallow cutback which was all that protected him. He succeeded to a degree. With infinite caution he raised his Colt to eye level, bobbed up six inches and blasted a shot at a dim shape above. He saw the slug strike rock and ricochet with a vicious whine before return fire saw him tuck his head in tighter than a sleeping sage hen, then peer cautiously out from beneath folded arms to see how the others were faring.

Hogue Kells lay belly flat behind the cover of his dead horse. The surviving punchers, wriggling and twisting, were doing their desperate best to conceal themselves deeper in a tangle of bramble and slough grass away to his right.

The dead waddy lay just as he had fallen, out in the open with one arm outflung and his face to the sky. He'd been chopped down in the first volley. The ambushers should have nailed more of them, Taller reflected with a kind of bitter satisfaction. They'd set up a smart trap, but over-eagerness had cost them a big tally.

A single Hightower rider had somehow scrambled away into a rocky draw downslope and gotten clear. Or so they hoped. The snipers had been pumping lead into the draw on and off ever since Curry vamoosed, and the survivors had seen or heard nothing of the waddy since. But Taller desperately wanted to believe the hand had made it all the way clear, then cut back to headquarters to get help. If they had a hope, that was it.

'Buck!' It was Flynn's voice.

'What?'

'They're moving down.'

With infinite caution, Taller raised his tousled head. For the moment he could see nothing but the glinting rifle barrel of an ambush gun protruding from the grey stone and brush of a hillside cleft. But as he continued to stare upwards, a figure leapt into sight, scuttled downwards some fifteen feet then dived behind a lichen-covered boulder the size of a hen house.

Ducking low once more he stared across at Kells' pale face. 'They ain't going to wait until dark, like I figured. They are fixing to finish us while it's still light.'

'Them and what army?'

Taller was startled by the other's defiance. Was it possible that second-rate Kells had more grit than he was given credit for?

'They don't need a freaking army,' he snarled back. 'They'll have us cold.'

'Take a look around. It's fifty feet to the base of the cliffs. We know they're coming and they ain't wearing armour. If we can't take 'em when they rush us – like they're going to have to do in the end – then we deserve what we get.'

It took some moments for a jangled Taller to realize his gun *segundo* was right. This should have made him feel good, but on the worst day of his life – and what might yet prove his last – his gunpacker's vanity was getting in the way of clear thinking. Demoted yesterday – now dumb Kells showing up better under fire than himself today. What next? Might he come apart altogether and end up blubbering and pleading for his life like a sick girl?

That thought steeled his backbone. He bobbed up and blasted two fast shots at the spot where the Cross-T shooter was last seen. Immediately a head bobbed into sight higher up, and Taller's snap shot caused a sombrero to fly into the air and it's owner to clutch his face and tumble backwards with a scream that jagged down the spine like a woodsaw blade.

'Got the bastard!' he triumphed. 'You see that, Kells? You are right, man, we can do it!'

'We're done for.'

'What?'

The face that turned towards him was now grey with fear. Kells had geared himself up briefly, but the ugly smack of Taller's bullet into human flesh had undone him again.

'Pull yourself together!' he snarled.

'Where in the Sam Hill are those wonder gunmen when a man wants them?' Kells bleated. 'I mean them big-money gunsharks from Chisum County. Where are they now? Hiding behind Miss Angie's skirts in the storm cellar if I'm any judge.'

Now Taller was glooming down again as he considered the situation as it stood.

'You know . . . Curry's had more than enough time to make it back to headquarters and bring help back with him. Guess we gotta face it now. He ain't coming and neither are they . . .'

His words were cut off abruptly as a slug whined viciously close, momentarily deafening him as it smacked a rock and ricocheted high.

General fire erupted from the cliffs and the defenders realized the enemy had improved their

44

attacking position as they worked their way lower. For several minutes the guns snarled back and forth like angry dogs, and the attack seemed to be faltering when a Hightower man was hit.

Clutching his shoulder, the man was belted from cover by the brutal impact of the high-powered bullet. Scrambling to hands and knees, he swung about and attempted to make it back to shelter before a hail of murderous lead chopped him down. With the horrified eyes of his henchmen staring out at him, the bronc stomper slumped flat, twitched convulsively and died.

Cross-T cheered. Hightower was silent. Neither Taller nor Kells was capable of any dramatic highs or lows any longer. Both men were now almost catatonic in the face of what looked like certain death. If they listened hard they could hear the rustling of bulky figures lowering themselves down behind the rock cover, drawing ever closer to their clearing. You could almost smell them now. It figured Cross-T could afford to soften them up some more when they were all in fresh positions, then simply close in whenever it suited and blow them away. Taller and Kells had always been second-raters. They were proving this to themselves, their cowboys and their enemies now. And the best Kells seemed able to come up with was a whimpering, 'I guess a man can only die once, Buck.'

'Why don't you die now, you whimpering heap of—'

Taller's voice faded. Under his right hand pressed against the bunch grass, he felt something. A pulsing, was his first guess. But then with a sudden chill, he thought, no. Not a pulsing. More like a trembling.

Horses?

The bastards were bringing in mounted reinforcements to finish them off!

He thought he screamed but it was only a whimper. But as he filled his lungs to shout – desperate to let the world hear the defiant voice of Buck Taller just one last time – the avalanching roar of concerted gunfire drowned out everything including even the rumbling thunder of steel-shod hoofs.

The gunman lay frozen in the foetal position waiting for the first Apocalyptic shape of man and horse to blot out his sky; waiting for the brutal fire-flash of the gun and the lead exploding his brain.

And waited.

Gradually he realized that the screaming, shouting and shooting, although fearsome in volume, were some distance away. Then through it all he heard a voice shout, 'Get that one, Trav!'

Trav?

A sixgun yammered, a man screamed in mortal agony. Then, 'By Judas, they don't make dirty sidewinding sons of bitches as tough as they used to, Chett!'

Taller jerked up and before him lay the vivid spectacle of some dozen Hightower horsemen surging to and fro across the clearing pouring a volley of scything lead into the cliff base where two dead and one badly wounded Cross-T man already lay bloody in the grass.

And Allison and Traven were doing most of the shooting.

'They've come!' he bleated, then dropped flat in an instant as a ricochet hummed close. It went swiftly from there.

Enemy riders were falling in the open as they attempted to flee to both east and west. Running was the worst thing they could have done. The second worst was to keep shooting as they retreated. A waddy dangling a bullet-shattered arm put a slug close to Allison's ugly horse. In response, three shots sounding like one boomed from Traven's right-hand Colt, and when the gunsmoke drifted the ambusher lay huddled in death.

'Surrender, muckers!' Traven bawled. But it was too late for that. As Taller's bunch had done before, the Cross-T fighters gave in to total panic. Three more dropped and suddenly the Hightower riders had nothing to shoot at but what remained of the enemy fleeing down the draw.

Allison raised his right hand to signal it was over, and cowboys lowered smoking guns. Not Traven. Teeth flashing in a savage grin, his expression demonic, the gunfighter raked savagely with spur to gallop headlong into the wooded draw where any cool-head with bullets in his gun could have chopped his huge figure down with ease.

There were no cool heads down there. As Hightower men checked the dead and wounded above, gunblasts rocked and roared below. But all came from the one set of Colts. Traven's.

By the time the man returned, grinning around a freshly lit cigar and heedless of a long bullet burn along his thigh, rescuers and rescued were resting, some even lighting up. They gaped as Traven reined in with a flourish before them, others grinned admiringly. Yet Allison's face was grim.

'Goddamn it, Trav, what'd you go do a fool thing like that for? They were finished. You could have got yourself killed down there!'

'Hell, this game's not worth a lick unless you push it to the limit.' Traven gestured at the scattered bodies. 'Anyways, they asked for it and they got what they asked for. Ain't that the rules we play by, man?'

A grim-faced Allison made no reply. But one of the rescued riders rushed forward and reached up to tearfully clutch Traven's hand. 'God bless you, Ned, we all thought we were done for and—'

Traven jerked his hand free roughly. 'Pull yourself together, cowpusher,' he snarled. 'This ain't any freakin' schoolgirls' outing. Get the hell away from me.'

There was a moment of silence as rescuers and rescued glanced from Traven to Allison in confusion. Allison's features remained blank while Traven just stared at them all with open contempt.

A thoughtful silence descended, dampening the exuberance of victory. Glances were exchanged. All on Hightower had been sharply aware of the striking differences between Allison and his gun *segundo* from the outset, but this was the first real insight they'd had into just how deep those differences actually might be. Chett Allison was seen as impressive by all – for a hired gun – but everyday working waddies were now realizing Traven might be cut from a vastly different cloth.

Allison stepped down, his voice filling the awkward silence which threatened to drag on.

'How many of you men hurt? Taller – is that blood on your shoulder?'

'Ain't nothing but a crease, Allison. But hell damn it, man, it was sure good to hear your guns opening up. I gotta say though, you showed just in the nick of time.'

'We'd been in position in back of the trees for ten minutes,' came the unexpected reply.

'Ten minutes? But why—?'

It was Traven who answered as he set a match to a cigar, spewing thick white smoke over his brutal underlip. He gestured.

'Why do you think, rube? One look told us how this turkey shoot was playing out. It was coming real gloomy and those muckers were creeping downhill, getting ready to rush you so soon as it was dark enough. If we'd have made our play while they were still holed up in the rocks, we could've lost men. Even worse, me or Chett might've stopped one, and where would that leave this lousy outfit?'

He paused to chuckle.

'So we done what any crackbrain would. We waited until they rushed out into the open . . . and damn me if it wasn't like picking off soda bottles in a shooting gallery, haw hah!'

'That man over there,' Allison cut in, indicating a crumpled Cross-T rider. 'He's not dead.'

Everybody turned at once. The bloodied figure, a smallish, hook-beaked man wearing leather shotgun chaps, raised his sorry head and groaned. Taller, grinning wolfishly, immediately pulled out his sixgun and lunged towards him.

'We'll soon cure that, by God!'

The man's actions were lightning fast, so fast, in fact, that Chett Allison had no option but to shoot first. His gun blazed away and the bullet whistled so close to Taller's jaw the man felt the heat of it. He flinched in shock and whirled, jaw agape, disbelieving.

'What in the tarnal did you do that for?'

Allison hammered down and holstered the smoking gun. 'Only a dog would shoot a helpless man, Taller.'

Traven's sardonic laughter broke the silence.

'Lets' face it, this just ain't your day, Taller. First you gallop into a booby-trap any ten-year old would have smelt out a mile away. Now you're showing the wide world what a low-life greenbelly you are on top of being stupid.'

Taller's face drained of colour. He was a genuine toughcase unaccustomed to mockery. Every instinct rebelled, yet he couldn't react, would not. Not here, not against this man. For both these men scared the tough gun, Traven even more so than Allison. To cover his humiliation before the onlookers he walked across to Allison who was checking out the injured enemy.

'He hurt bad, Allison?'

'Nope.' Allison straightened. 'A clean wound on the upper back, is all.' He nodded to a couple of waddies nearby. 'Get him on to a horse.'

The men hastened to obey, hustling off to the

horses which had been tied up since the shooting stopped. Taller studied Allison curiously.

'What do you plan to do with this jasper?'

'Take him to the medic in town. What else? Matter of fact, you can escort him in. You can both see him together.'

'But, Judas Priest, he's Cross-T. Ten minutes back he was trying to kill us.'

'You're responsible for his safety,' Allison replied curtly as he turned on his heel and walked away.

Taller bit back the retort. The exhilaration of their hair's-breadth escape was fading fast. Just a week earlier he'd been top hand on the spread, now he was just some kind of whipping boy to Hannibal's prize gun studs. Maybe the best thing to do for now was simply shut up and do as ordered.

He shivered suddenly. It was quite dark and cold now and for the first time he realized just how much his wound hurt.


'Got 'em set up, Chett,' Traven boomed as Allison pushed through the batwings of the Indian Queen. 'All right you broken-winded bindle-stiffs, make way for my pard. And keep your distance. If there's one thing he can't stomach it's crawlers and leeches who wanna be his friend. Move, I said!'

They moved.

Allison made his slow way to the bar as Traven turned and winked broadly at a busty percentage girl seated at a nearby table with a couple of local businessmen.

'See, told you he'd be coming, honey.' Then he

scowled. 'But don't bother coming sucking around him neither. We're still resting up from shooting up folks, and that sure takes it out of a man.' Then he winked again. 'But don't break your heart. I'll get around to you later, and you know what I mean.'

Then he turned as Allison hefted his glass, raised his own and said, 'How!'

'How, Trav.'

They drank and the Indian Queen was quiet. The dead had been laid to rest that morning and there were mourners present in Buffalo Gate's biggest saloon. The cowtown had grown accustomed to gunpackers and their violent ways as the range war worsened, but the clash at Tumbleweed Ridge had been the worst yet by far, chalking up the largest loss of life to date.

The county had been abuzz with rumour and unease ever since the shootout and nobody seemed to know what might be the outcome other than that Cross-T Ranch could not and would not allow the bloody defeat to go unanswered. But this seemed of little concern to the two tall men leaning on the long bar beneath the hanging lamps. Traven, laughing and joking, might have been a harmless cowboy out for a night's fun, while Allison appeared – or so thought those men and women who were seeing him for the first time – more like a banker or high-rolling businessman relaxing after a hard day. But for the guns, of course.

With four sixguns between them and dead men behind them already, there could be no forgetting just who and what these men were.

'Didn't see you at the buryings, Chett,' Traven remarked with a sly grin.

'That's because I wasn't there.' Allison sipped at his glass of Green River bourbon. 'Neither were you.'

'How'd you figure?' Traven asked.

Allison indicated the blonde. 'You haven't surfaced for twenty-four hours, is why.'

'Why, you sneaky varmint, you've had your spies watching me.'

Allison smiled but didn't deny the charge. When a man rode with a gun partner like Ned Traven, he took precautions. Traven might well be the best backup man in the business, but the other side of the gunfighter and man could scare a snake.

This was a thought that raised an unresolved matter.

Traven was talking fast when Allison suddenly broke in. 'What are you doing here, Ned?'

Traven blinked. 'Huh? What does it look like? I'm doing what you're doing, easing off after the shootup and having a few stiff shots. What sort of dumb-ass question is that?'

Allison met his stare on the level.

'You know what I mean. What are you doing here in Vulcan County right now?'

Traven paled. He began to bluster but the other held up a silencing hand.

'Hannibal hired me, Trav. He contacted me, we agreed on terms and I quit Fort Union alone. Yet when I got to the spread, you were already there ahead of me. How come?'

'Damnit, you're talking ancient history, man. That

53

was all yesterday, last week. How come you're griping about it now?'

Allison shook his head slowly.

'Trav, I know you love the game, and I'll never deny I owe you plenty. But after our last job I thought we agreed to split. I mean, I'm a loner by nature and you're . . . you're . . .'

'C'mon,' Traven said, grim-faced now. 'What am I, Chett?'

Allison looked away, jaw muscles working.

'You're somebody who enjoys it all too much, is what. I told you that after the wagon train escort we did to Oxtail. You shot people who didn't have to die, Trav. And that wasn't the first time. I reckoned then it was best we split, I still think it. Sorry, but that's the way it is.'

It seemed a long taut time before a pale Ned Traven found his voice.

'So, you want me to quit? Hell, we've seen what we're up against here, and you said yourself this dogfight's gonna get worse afore it gets better. Damn it all, man, the least I can do is stick it out for this job at least.' He forced a grin. 'They breed backshooters here. Who's gonna watch your back while you trim them down to size? Have you seen one Hannibal hand or any of their so-called supporters who you could rely on to watch a baby didn't swallow its goddamn dummy? You wanna die here in this dump? Is that it?'

Allison looked away.

This was a tough spot he was in.

Traven was as loyal as they came and a master with

54

the guns. But there was a worrying other side. It seemed as time went by the man was growing wilder and less predictable, and the burden of riding with somebody who could sometimes seem more dangerous than any enemy was weighing him down.

He wanted to wind up the partnership now. Just as he knew he wanted to hang up his guns finally at the end of the colonel's job.

First get rid of Traven, then quit at job's end. Sounded simple. But when forced to meet the other's gaze, the guilt kicked in. He still owed Ned. He might try and convince himself otherwise, but that was plain truth.

He realized he couldn't rightly call it quits, mid job. He'd have to do it right.

'OK,' he sighed, placing the empty glass on the bar. 'So, I admit I need you behind me here.' He looked up. 'But that's it, Trav. After we're through here we ride different trails—'

'We'll talk about that then, *amigo*. Have another.'

'Sorry, got an appointment.' He saluted and said, 'How.'

'How.'

Later the drinkers watched Allison's tall figure thread its way between the tables. Then attention switched to Traven, who poured a double which he sank at one gulp. The blonde rose from her table and crossed to the bar. She said something and Traven backhanded her, spilling her to the floor. The bartender exploded with rage and lunged across the bar swinging a beer bung. Traven blocked the blow with his forearm, got a grip on the man with his free hand and dragged him over the bar. He drove a knee into his guts as he fell.

'Who the freak is next?' he shouted, and there was a hushed intake of breath as they saw the gun glittering in his hand. 'All right!' he said, holstering the piece and spreading hands wide. 'Now – anybody?'

No takers.

The silence held and deepened until Traven booted a table out of his path and went lunging from the smoke-filled room, almost taking the swinging doors off their hinges as he surged out into the night.

Drinkers rushed to help the dazed couple as neighbour stared dumbly at neighbour in total confusion. Up until five minutes ago, Buffalo Gate had hoped that the range war, which was badly affecting them all, might be within sight of resolution thanks to the brutal efficiency of Hightower's new gun force.

Few townsfolk were aligned with one spread or the other.

All folks craved was peace and fewer funerals. Allison and Traven had seemed to fill the role of the genuine peacekeepers which the region had not been able to attract from any other source up until now, and most of the town and country had been ready to cheer them on to victory – until roughly five minutes ago.

That had been all the time it took to sense that Chett Allison and Ned Traven might not be what they'd appeared at first sighting. Allison seemed OK, likely the best prospect for Buffalo Gate. But how did you figure his *segundo*? Traven was already beginning

to shape up as the kind of hellion whom even someone as ruthless as Wolf Stobaugh might balk at
hiring, yet here he was riding for the Hannibal
brand.

Soon everyone began talking at once, and everyone had an opinion. There didn't seem to be a single
citizen now who believed other than that, instead of
the general situation improving, as all had desperately hoped for, it might easily turn uglier than
anyone might have feared.

They sensed the Hightower cure could prove
worse than the complaint.

# CHAPTER 4

# A TOWN AFRAID

The clash between Cross-T and Hightower at Tumbleweed Ridge set the torch to the tinderbox across Vulcan County's hills and green valleys.

Forty-eight hours after that battle – barely long enough to bury the dead – Cross-T riders struck the southern plains of Hightower in force, putting several herders to flight and badly wounding another in a lightning raid that resulted in the successful run-off of seventy head of Colonel Hannibal's prime breeding stock.

Hightower struck back at dawn next day, stampeding a gather two miles deep in enemy land and leaving one man dead and another wounded in the carnage they left in their dust.

The five days following were reminiscent of the savage skirmishing that went on behind the lines of battle during the War, yet this was peace-time Nevada and not bloody Georgia or Tennessee.

During that week Chett Allison and Ned Traven earned their fees a dozen times over. In the saddle day and night, singly or together, they constantly swept the immense high plateau reaches of the Hightower, the target for snipers' guns and survivors of a dozen skirmishes.

The gunfighters' experience with such conditions as much as their gunskills and reputations seemed to armour-plate them against enemy guns, while casualties escalated in the enemy camp.

Chett Allison seemed shaped by nature to play out the role of gunmaster supreme in this deadly environment, as was usually the case wherever he plied his trade. He fitted the picture with his impressive appearance and courtly manner backed up by an uncanny ability with twin sixguns, attributes which were complemented by his talent for getting along easily with most everyone from the colonel down to the cook's louse. This gunman stood tall. But time and success failed to gild his gun partner with the same kind of aura.

In that same testing time period, Ned Traven affirmed the bad impression he'd created in just that handful of brutal moments at the Indian Queen Saloon. Had a straw poll been taken on Hightower to identify the most disliked man in the county, he may have only run second to Wolf Stobaugh, but not by much.

Arrogant and patronizing, the gunfighter rode roughshod over virtually everybody with the exception of just two whom he treated with unfailing respect, Chett Allison and Angelina Hannibal.

Nobody questioned the man's ability or courage, but this still won few admirers. Riding with Traven, a man never knew when he might decide to pull some crazy-brave kind of stunt and expect you to back his play and so run the risk of getting shot into doll rags, seemingly for no real purpose.

At times men on Hightower feared Traven more than they did Wolf Stobaugh's gun crew. And early on, the obvious question arose in the ranks. Namely, how come a straight-shooter like Allison rode tandem with such a man?

Nobody could figure, not in the bunkhouse nor beneath the gilded chandeliers of the ranch house.

But as somebody remarked, this was war, not a popularity contest.

Day after day the colonel's new guns saddled up to lead Hightower against the enemy, and each night, reviewing the dangerous day behind them, the ranch riders were forced to acknowledge the fact that it had to be the best step Hannibal had ever done when he put himself into debt and hired Allison and his partner, warts and all.

It was during this brutal testing period that the war seriously spilled over into Buffalo Gate for the first time.

The sheriff, a middle-aged peace officer who'd done his best to confine the conflict to the rangeland, was shown to be virtually powerless when bullets began to fly within the town limits, destroying its reputation as the unofficial no-man's-land it had enjoyed for so long.

It had to happen.

Too many people had died, and men filled with hate and a thirst for vengeance were prone to come face to face on the streets with men who just the day previous had torn down a fence, taken a shot at them or set the torch to their hay barn or feed lot.

In the wake of the first town shootout it became almost commonplace for guns to flare in a darkened alleyway or a vacant lot, and soon all Buffalo Gate was being drawn into the conflict.

With the sheriff virtually a prisoner in his own jail-house, no help from the capital, as usual, and with no response to Buffalo Gate's county-wide advertisement for deputies, it was a miracle that no citizen actually lost his life in that stretch of time. However, several men were wounded, some seriously, and the threat was always there. So, without a peace officer or official worthy of the name to appeal to whenever a citizen might be threatened, shot-up or chased out of town, the last resort for the harried people of Buffalo Gate was their own territorial representative, Mr Belden Harte.

Harte was a smooth unflappable man with a golden moustache and impeccable manners. 'I'm sorry, Mr Jones,' he said regretfully in his office above the Buffalo Gate Council Chambers that blustery day with fog clinging to the valleys, 'but your problem is simply not of sufficient magnitude to warrant my passing it on to my superiors in the capital.'

'But,' protested the whiskery hog butcher, 'them damn drunks shot three of my prize sows and then—'

'Regrettable, Mr Jones. Now, if you'll excuse me, I have others awaiting an audience.'

'But—'

'Thank you, Mr Jones!'

'Fat lot of good you're likely to do in there,' ripe-smelling Jones complained to the group lounging, standing by the windows of the ante room as he stomped for the stairs.

'You heard about Nero fiddlin' while Rome burned? This geezer makes him look like a civic-minded citizen by comparison.'

Cussing and fuming, one disgruntled taxpayer vanished down the stairs as Belden Harte appeared in his office doorway with his smooth smile firmly in place.

'Ah, come through, Mr Stobaugh. Alone, if you please.'

Wolf Stobaugh scowled and said, 'What about my brother, Mr Harte?'

The government man arched an eyebrow at the slender youth, who in no physical way resembled his bearded, ox-shouldered brother, the boss of Cross-T Ranch.

'Er, I'm afraid not, Casey. I'm sure you don't mind?'

Casey Stobaugh minded like hell. Although a year shy of his twentieth birthday, and weighing less than 140 pounds, Wolf's kid brother was a hothead with a reputation and a quick temper which frequently led him into trouble from which only big brother could extricate him, either by brute force, bribery or some-times both.

He looked ready to erupt, but Wolf held up a warning finger. 'Go get something to eat with the boys.' The finger wagged. 'Now!'

The Cross-T party clattered downstairs and Harte ushered his visitor through to the inner sanctum. Only then did the man from the capital shed his smooth public persona like a cloak as he hauled a bottle of whiskey and two glasses from a cabinet and began to pour.

'Well, let's hear it, Wolf. All of it.'

'There's good and bad, Bel.'

Despite the status that his position as one of the county's two biggest cattlemen gave him, citizens who knew Stobaugh would have been astonished to witness the easy familiarity displayed towards Nevada's top official in Vulcan County, or Harte's towards him.

Neither man was congenial by nature and neither sought or cultivated friendships, as a rule.

There were also the personality differences to consider. Belden Harte was a highly educated gentleman of achievement accustomed to mixing in the best of official circles, while Wolf Stobaugh was a bullying brute whose only identifiable common trait with the government man was ambition.

Stobaugh wanted it all and so did Harte.

It had been the pair's initial recognition of a common characteristic in each other that had first brought them together.

Realizing almost by instinct just how much they thought, acted and dreamed alike, their fast-firing partnership had resulted in dramatic changes in their lives for both men, changes that would profoundly affect them both in time, along with the entire county.

It was a partnership laden with risk, and cost.

For Wolf Stobaugh the tie-up entailed draining his resources to a dangerous low to finance his ever-widening campaign to bring his Hightower rival to his knees. For his part, Belden Harte found himself prepared to risk ruin and even possibly prison by conniving secretly and illicitly against his distant masters, the law of the land. But even more astonishingly, this man of hitherto impeccable reputation now found himself embezzling funds from his governmental employers in order to keep the feud blazing. Stobaugh still sometimes awoke in his big brass bed out on the spread to sit up, scratch his ragged mane and marvel at the mystery of how he'd hit it off with such a figure in the land as Harte. But day by day he was realizing that behind his high-toned ways and the fancy uniforms he decked himself out in for major civic occasions – Belden Harte was, underneath, every bit as ruthless and ambitious a son of a bitch as himself. Up until a year ago, Belden Harte had actually been the reliable, honest public servant and man of important government affairs as everyone believed him to be.

He was then the happily wed under-secretary to the governor and considered himself a happy man on the way up. Then his lady wife, without warning, left him for a former high government official, a friend of Harte's who'd been dismissed in disgrace for offences ranging from accepting bribes to falsifying government contracts, even embezzlement.

Everyone including Harte expected his wife's lover to go to jail. Instead the prosecution fouled up their case and the man got off without charge. One month later, accompanied by Martha Harte, he left for Europe for a two-year vacation, deluxe all the way.

That was the moment when the iron entered Harte's soul and he sat up all one night with a fifth of Old Savanna bourbon muttering, 'Honesty is for suckers.'

His wife's lover had made his illicit fortune, not in Carson City, but in what he referred to as 'the provinces', meaning the outer counties.

Six weeks later a totally transformed Harte had his application for the position of official representative in Buffalo Gate, Vulcan County, approved.

If one government man could make his fortune far from the close scrutiny of the capital, he attested, so could another.

Within a week of his arrival he had acquired as broad an understanding of the feud as any local, a week after that he was introduced to Wolf Stobaugh – and was on his way. Within a week the two men were working in tandem under cover of the range war to achieve the identifiable goal, the bringing down of Colonel Hannibal and the eventual takeover of Hightower Ranch. After this was achieved they planned to become legal partners in the ownership of the resulting affiliation of the two spreads which would create the biggest cattle ranch in the state of Nevada.

For weeks now the partners had been riding high.

But not so today. They were sober and grim as they took chairs on opposite sides of Harte's impressive desk to consider yet again the worsening, unforeseen problem that had first caught them napping when Lawson Hannibal dug deep and hired himself two renowned troubleshooters from the north, to take up residence on Hightower for what was believed to be an indefinite period.

The fact that Harte and Stobaugh believed the colonel was risking financial ruin in meeting Allison's high fees on top of his other greatly enhanced war expenses, had given the two some brief comfort. But this had only lasted until the recent clash at Tumbleweed Ridge which had brought a chill wind of fear blowing through this place, and for the first time the plotters seriously considered the possibility that they could lose, after all.

Harte wanted good news today; Stobaugh gave him what he had.

'Well, you'll like this, Belden. My top gun, Seneca McVey, has been able to recruit some of his kinfolk guns who'll be showing up by the end of the week. You heard of a gunpacker name of Cash Slattery?' The other nodded and he went on. 'Got him at a good price. And that feller's just rearing to carve a big name for himself up here.'

'And what else?'

'Well, four of our boys quit after the funerals. Lily-livered sons of bitches. McVey's men will boost us, but will likely only bring us back up to the strength we were before.' The big man broke off to curse.

'Those Hightower imports are hurting us bad, Bel, no two ways about it. One of 'em's got folks believing he's some kind of hero, the other shapes as about the meanest gun snake this county's ever seen.'

'I'm not interested in hearing what I already know. What are you doing to counter Allison and Traven? What can we do together?'

They debated their mutual problem for some time before moving on to general tactics and how they might be best employed. Stobaugh seemed cheered and strengthened by the time he left the office, and Harte saw him off with a big grin that vanished the moment the door closed on the six-footer's wide back.

The man who was now virtually the mastermind behind the Hightower-Cross-T range war, poured himself another stiff one and toted it to the window overlooking the timber yard next door, deep in thought now.

'Allison and Traven . . .' he muttered before taking a jolt.

He'd minimized their importance to his partner, but was too astute to deceive himself. So Hannibal had risked ruin by hiring one of the priciest guns in the territory? So what? It could prove the best investment the man ever made should Hightower come out top dog.

And of course, he reflected sourly, luck had boosted Hannibal when, in hiring Allison, he scored the unexpected bonus of Allison's gun pard showing up to scare the daylights out of almost everyone, resulting in a worsening situation that Belden Harte knew he must correct fast before Wolf's 'good and bad' news got to be all bad. He nodded firmly now, recognizing what must be done. Never mind waiting for Hannibal to go bust, or for Lady Luck to chime in on their side. There was but one solution, so he saw with crystal clarity for the first time. It was so obvious he'd almost overlooked it.

Chett Allison had to go, no matter what the cost.

Easier in his own mind now the decision was made, he stared across the street at the saloon where Stobaugh would be drinking and bragging with his men – and gave himself over to the luxury of his favourite daydream. The one in which the Hannibals and Allison were just a memory and he and Wolf Stobaugh were co-owners of the one giant cattle empire.

The documents establishing this partnership and identifying its intentions, restrictions and legal parameters had already been drawn up, signed before a notary public and placed in the bank vault for safe-keeping.

The papers had been drafted by Belden Harte's attorney, a man with a real genius for turning out documentation that could, when necessary, almost convince that black was white. The man could even conceal a hideously inappropriate clause or condition by burying it under language that made it read like harmless word spinning.

This document with Wolf Stobaugh's untidy signature scrawled on the last page contained a cunningly worded clause which stipulated that, in the event of the demise of one or other partner, the combined ranches would become the sole property of the survivor.

Harte smiled. Accidents could happen. Often did. To anybody. Even a big strong ox like Wolf Stobaugh.

His smile became a chuckle. It paid to remind himself of the pot at the end of the rainbow every so often.

It would be a long time before Belden Harte would feel this confident again.


Ned Traven's swaggering figure emerged from under the striped canopy slung over the entrance to the barn. A red-headed cowhand toting a big Spanish saddle wandered by, nodded with just the right blend of respect and wariness. The sun was out for a change. The Hightower morning was crisp and bright with hardy scavenger birds fighting over scraps in back of the cookshack on a morning still innocent of alarms or calls to arms. Traven was grinning as he strode across the big ranch yard, but nobody he encountered smiled back.

The gunfighter was respected here but not liked. He knew it, revelled in it, at times seemed to go out of his way to exacerbate it.

Yet despite this generally hostile attitude which prevailed all the way from the house gallery where Angelina Hannibal stood watching with one hand shielding her eyes against the unfamiliar sun, to the bunkhouse steps where weary cowhands stretched and yawned, there was a countering reassurance for the onlookers as they watched him flexing his shoulders then aim a kick that missed at a yellow rooster which strayed too close.

No doubt about it; it was comforting to have this man about regardless of his shortcomings. And these days that counted for a lot.

'High there, bright-eyes!'

Angelina nodded gravely. He didn't scare her, mainly because she was strong, and also because he continued to treat her like the lady she was. The girl's gaze followed him as he legged it by for the stables where she saw a boy grooming his fine black saddler with a hair brush.

She knew Traven was showing off for her benefit when he thrust the boy aside, vaulted astride the animal bareback and kicked it around the yard with his heels.

Suddenly he jerked on the glossy mane and guided the horse across to the hedge encircling the house.

'Something to see eh?' he grinned, drawing up. 'Fine specimen of manhood forking a smart looking horse. Wanna double up bareback?'

She actually smiled. The situation on the ranch wavered between grim and dangerous these days, with clashes with Cross-T almost a daily occurrence. There were men with gunshot wounds, her father pacing his study floor until late into the night, gunfighters wandering around the place at large almost as if they were normal men in a sensible world. Angelina was strong, yet she often yearned for the days when a big grin wasn't a rarity, even if this one's was not to be trusted.

'I'm not sure father would approve.'

'Fathers never approve nothing pretty daughters

wanna do. That's a Traven fact of life.'

'Tell me something,' she said, moving across to the hedge. 'How is it you ride such a fine horse while Chett's looks more like a hack?'

'Just don't seem right, does it?'

'Well. . . ?'

'It's a tad embarrassing. . . .'

'I'm listening.'

'Well, I kinda did Chett a favour once, and he made me take his horse and insisted on riding mine.'

'What was the favour?'

'You are one nosy lady, know that?'

'Don't be shy. It doesn't suit you.'

'I kinda saved his life.'

'Oh, I see. . . .'

'And what do you mean by that, bright-eyes?' he demanded suspiciously. His gaze narrowed. 'Ah, I get it. You're figuring, in that pretty head of yours, that he'd have to have a real good reason before he could stomach someone like me around.'

'I wasn't thinking anything of the sort.'

'Well, we'd have probably been pards even if he didn't feel he owes me. He's the kind of guy who just naturally has got a soft spot for freaks. You know . . . cripples or bums or crazies that nobody else'll have anything to do with.' His smile was savage. 'Or hadn't you noticed?'

'At times you make it very hard to have a conversation with you, Mr Traven. I'm sure that—'

But Traven wasn't listening. Traven kicked the horse away to go cantering around the yard, leaving her pensive.

In the period the two men from the north had been riding for Hightower the colonel's daughter had studied them with the intensity of an anthropologist confronted with the strangest of strange specimens. Still innocently unaware of just how much time she spent watching or thinking about Chett Allison, she had continued to be puzzled by the unlikely pairing they made.

Now she wondered if she mightn't be beginning to understand, after all. She was convinced Allison was a gentleman, if anything but a 'gentle man.' It was highly possible, she reasoned, that a man like that would take the saving of his life very seriously, perhaps seriously enough to go to the lengths of allowing a man he owed to tag along with him out of gratitude.

That would explain the mystery of the Allison-Traven partnership.

Now she could concentrate on other important matters and plans.

Satisfied with her reasoning, she mounted the steps and walked down the breezeway to the cross corridor which she took to the west wing, where her father and breakfast were waiting.

'What's that man doing out there?' Hannibal greeted her; she knew whom he meant.

'Nothing offensive.'

'That's a change.' Hannibal mashed ham and bacon together, loaded up his fork, then paused. 'And where's Prince Charming?'

'My, we are in a mood today. If you mean Mr Allison, I haven't see him and—'

'Someone mention my name?'

The gunfighter entered the room, clean-shaven, string tie, black coat. He halted with a nod to Angelina then turned to her father. 'I'm told you wanted to see me?'

'Correct. Please join us, and Millie will fetch you some breakfast.'

Allison complied and the older man fixed him with a sharp eye. 'Tactics,' he said. 'This morning I want to discuss tactics.'

'Perhaps I should leave you together?' Angelina suggested.

'No,' Allison said quickly.

'Perhaps it would be best at that,' the rancher demurred.

'No, it wouldn't, Colonel. Your daughter's no child. She's grown up with this damned war. Whatever we say isn't going to shock her any.'

Angelina smiled. Hannibal's eyes glinted momentarily, then went dull. The 'damned war' was grinding him down despite the fact that at the moment they seemed to be winning it.

'You could be right,' he muttered. 'So, let's get started. . . .'

# CHAPTER 5

## GUNMAN AT BAY

From a cane-bottomed chair on the verandah of the County Hotel, Ned Traven sat watching Buffalo Gate in the afternoon. A fuming cigar jutted from his teeth. His legs were crossed and his elevated fancy boots rested comfortably against a timber roof support. He appeared relaxed, but who could be sure about that? He was amused when pedestrians came strolling by – soaking up a feeble little piece of winter sunshine and plainly contented enough with their own dreary little lives in a back country hick town – before they sighted him.

He grinned around his cheroot.

Sometimes they just tucked their chins in and hurried on by, the odd one nodding amiably enough but by far the greater number just looking jittery, as rightly they should.

Not much was happening in town today. There was talk going round that Wolf Stobaugh's gunman;

Seneca McVey, was bringing in some fast-shooting kinsmen any day now, the intention being to regain the top hold which Cross-T had enjoyed, prior to him and Chett coming by to snatch it away from them.

He yawned and stretched.

He was as good as certain that McVey's crummy cousins would prove to be no better than McVey himself, whom he classed as a bona fide second-rater. But he tried to be optimistic. There was one named Slattery, who might have some talent. He hoped the man had loads of gunskills and came overloaded with aggression. It was three days since he'd shot anybody and he worried he might rust up if he didn't get some action soon.

A familiar face drifted into his line of vision.

The sheriff averted his face and hurried on. A sneer curled Traven's lip. What a failure! Small wonder things had gotten out of hand here with a loser like that bossing the law office.

With a sigh he tilted his chair back, hauled his right hand sixgun, broke it open then held the muzzle to his eye and squinted down the dark mirror shine of the barrel. Clean as a hound's tooth.

Of course, he knew it would be. He was just making a show in the hope of maybe stirring something up.

He scowled and housed the weapon, falling prey to an old familiar discontent. He knew the symptoms. If he didn't keep moving he tended to sink into himself, like he was doing right now.

All of a sudden he seemed to settle and grow weary with the old melancholy feeling of not understanding himself or the clay that made him. His gaze turned inwards and the swaggering extrovert was replaced by a perception of himself as something dark and sick.

He flinched a little and flicked ash off his cheroot.

It was times like this that pumped-up bravado and raging aggression deserted him and he began scrambling around trying to identify in himself qualities or virtues such as other men had, some by the cart-load.

He failed, and the panic began to settle in. He dropped his boots and stared at the floorboards as he fought to come out of the self-induced introspection.

Was he just nothing?

That was his great secret fear, the thing that at times made him do things he couldn't understand – the suspicion that his whole life added up to a tally of meaningless years and insane violence, and that he, Edward James Traven, was a creature without one solitary virtue and therefore unfit to live.

Then, almost too late, through his mental fog, he saw the life-raft and grabbed it. He was Chett's friend!

How could you forget that, you idiot, just because you're feeling overhung and sorry for yourself?

He opened his eyes and blinked, almost smiling. That was the one understanding that could always drag him out of his black pit. Chett Allison was a good man and a hero, and Ned Traven was his friend. That meant he must be worthwhile after all, and was six kinds of a fool ever to doubt it.

Now his smile grew broad and his barrel chest began to swell. The day was bright again and he knew he would be just fine until the next time his secret fears stalked him and laid him low.

'What do you reckon, Cash? Does this look like some kind of world-beater or more like some old bum who dozes off in the sun and don't bother nobody until his potty needs emptying?'

The voice seemed to come from a great distance, alerting Traven that his head was still far from clear. He blinked in the sunlight and tried to focus, feeling the onset of the headache that always followed a hard drinking session compounded by one of his huge depressions.

The voice again, clearer now.

'Got him figured yet, Cousin?'

'Not sure if I have or not, Seneca . . . .'

Traven's eyes widened. Seneca? Could be only one man with a handle like that in this town. Seneca McVey – Stobaugh gun!

The whiff of trouble cleared his vision as quickly as it had clouded over and he was on his feet, sucking air into his chest and rearranging the aggressive set of his jaw as he sighted the danger.

It stood directly before him by the hitchrail. No less than five men wearing guns, two or three he identified as Cross-T, including a well set-up gentleman who wore a single Remington butt-forward on his right hip, Seneca McVey.

This could be real trouble!

It couldn't have shown at a better time.

In an instant Traven was whole again, as he knew he must be. The grey veil was gone and his fingers tingled as he moved to the top of the steps, presenting a big target if anybody had the guts to go for it.

Hostile eyes met his. He met McVey's stare with a bleak warning, then flicked his gaze to the skinny, wild-eyed kid he knew to be Casey Stobaugh. Some claimed that Wolf's kid brother was half-touched and dangerous.

He'd not sighted the thick-necked man in the red shirt before and guessed he could be the new gunny, Cash Slattery. He'd dimly heard the name 'Cash' in his stupor, sensed it had likely been Casey Stobaugh's voice making the smart remarks.

Something subtle happened to Traven's eyes. He flashed a savage grin at them as he halted at the base of the steps. When his power returned after unsettling interludes like this, it did so in a rush.

'Must be getting old,' he said, feeling the old familiar excitement. 'Thought I heard voices. You know, a crackly, corny kinda hick voice like it had leaked outta some weedy kid with eyes like crab apples and no balls at all. But I don't see nobody around here measures up to that, so I guess I must've been dreaming.'

Young Stobaugh took a step forward but the stranger with the thick neck grabbed him and drew him back.

The kid was furious.

'Let me at him, Cash!' he panted. 'He don't scare me and never did. He's a nothing. I can take the bastard – we can!'

People were stopping in the street to watch and shopkeepers appeared in their doorways, wary yet attracted by the whiff of trouble.

These were no more than a peripheral blur to

Traven. He was totally focused on the men before him. Locked in. Sure, he'd given his word at the spread he wouldn't raise any dust in town, but that was before this dog pack ganged up on him.

Likely they'd spotted him when he was out of it – going to the mat with his demons. Bastards should have jumped when they had half a chance.

His fingers were tingling and he was trying to decide if he should take out the new man first – his hot blood could carry him away to that extent.

He lifted his hands, palms upwards and beckoned with curling fingers.

'Come on, kid. Guys out at Hightower claim we ought treat you like a joke and just ignore you, like an underfed pup without a brain in its skull. But I wouldn't insult a fire-eater like you by not taking you serious. This is man-to-man stuff, and if you want to haul that hogleg fastened to your hip, why I'll be obliged to give you satisfaction.'

'Judas Priest, he's only a kid,' McVey protested. 'Anyways, it was only jawbone, Traven. He never meant anything by it.'

Traven threw his head back and laughed.

'Hell, nor did I, Mac. You think a big ugly geezer like me would really haul iron on a kid? No chance.'

As he spoke he was easing forward. Suddenly he was quite close to Stobaugh, so close in fact that two lunging strides took him to the youth and his looping right fist blurred and smacked jaw with a sound like an axe biting into wet wood. The kid's eyes rolled as he was driven back senseless into those behind, arms flailing, blood stuttering through his teeth.

Traven went after him and Cash Slattery stuck out a boot and tripped him up.

He went down on his elbows.

Instantly a bootheel smashed into his temple, stunning him. He was seeing double as he struggled to rise, but in an instant they were rushing in on all sides. Cross-T had had no prior plan to take on Allison's *segundo*. This had erupted spontaneously, and boosted by new blood they recognized an advantage they couldn't resist.

'Let's finish the bastard!' screamed Casey Stobaugh, coming out of it, and a slamming knee caught the side of the gunfighter's spinning head as he again attempted to muscle his way to his feet.

Traven rolled from the impact and felt the acid taste of alarm in his mouth as he flung up powerful arms to protect his head.

Foolishly, carelessly, he'd let himself be suckered into a potentially desperate situation.

Sure, he had his guns. But if gunplay should erupt the odds were five-to-one against in an up-close and fluid situation which could virtually negate gunspeed or skill.

He might take out two or three. But these men were all gunners. One or two might even be genuine class, meaning if he hauled iron it might well be the last thing he ever did.

He couldn't believe he'd let himself be suckered in, blamed it on his crazy mood swing. They always drained him and left him vulnerable – if such a word could ever be used to describe him.

Getting to his knees, he collected a solid blow to

the mouth and retaliated with a vicious hook that connected with a man's ear and sent him spinning.

With a tremendous burst of strength he finally surged erect. Slattery's powerful features blurred in his vision. He seized the man by both ears and bashed his head into his face. Blood flew and next instant Traven was doubling over in agony as a pistoning bootheel found his groin.

Unable to straighten, he tried to weave, attempted to backtrack to the porch. They wouldn't let him, and suddenly he felt the weight of his .45 leave his right hip. Desperate now, he clawed for his second gun, gasped as teeth sunk into the side of his reaching hand.

The pain maddened him. With both heavy arms fully extended now, he spun on the spot, the windmilling effect of flailing arms belting two men off their feet, giving him one brief surge of hope.

Then something hard slammed the back of his head with stunning force and he was face down in the street, spitting mud and crud until someone dropped on to his back with both knees driving into his kidneys and driving the last ounce of breath from tortured lungs.

The encircling line of legs blurred in his vision and his mouth was filled with blood. 'Rubes!' he choked. And he couldn't believe any of it, not the pain, the helplessness or the realization that it all might be ending this way.

He knew he was sinking fast when he could no longer feel their blows or hear them cursing. His head swam as he gasped for air. He attempted to roll over and to his intense surprise, was permitted to do so. Weakly he slung his right arm over his face for protection against the blows – that didn't come. Cautiously he lowered his arm. The legs still encircled him, but it was their backs he was staring at now.

And through a gap, the blurred figure astride a bullet-headed grulla.

Allison nodded when he saw Traven lift his head, then returned his attention to the line of panting Cross-T brawlers. The bunch had fallen silent the moment he appeared out of Riddle Alley, some backing up quickly in expectation of gunplay. But Allison's hands stayed clear of his weapons as he drew his mount to a halt and said quietly, yet in a tone that carried. 'Get!'

Wolf Stobaugh made to move off but his kid brother seized him by the elbow.

'What the hell are you doing, Wolf? He ain't law. We got as much right to—'

He broke off with a sudden choking sound as Allison kneed his horse forward. The kid tried to jump clear but was sent flying as the animal's shoulder hit him hard.

'Why you mongrel b—' Slattery began, dropping his hand close to his gun. Then froze. Allison sat his saddle with his hands crossed on the pommel, his eyes cold blue.

'Try it and I'll kill you!' Chett's voice filled the street. He waited until the gunman jerked his hand away from his gun and backed up, before making a sweeping gesture with his right hand. 'Clear the street. This has gone as far as it's going.' His voice rose. 'I mean now!'

The spectacle of five dangerous men staring uncertainly at one another, before big Stobaugh turned and started off west along the street, was impressive. Yet more unusual and unexpected was the sound that came, hesitant at first, but slowly increasing in volume as the street noises diminished – of someone clapping. Allison turned his head sharply in the direction of the sound. The applauder was a plump town matron in a quaker cloth dress. As he stared, someone across the street put his hands together, to be supported by another and another until half Federation Street was joining in.

It took a moment or two for Allison to realize what was happening. The citizens of Buffalo Gate might well be admiring what he'd done. Yet to him it was crystal clear from their appearance that what they were really applauding was the fact that a situation that might have exploded into chaos had been averted.

The man in the street who'd watched helplessly as the range war had begun invading his town had feared the ruckus between Traven and the Cross-T must have a bloody outcome. Now it was over, and some might have even been moved to cheer as a bloody-faced Traven staggered to his feet, had it been just about anybody but him. Traven had no friends in Buffalo Gate, but that wasn't the same as saying he was without a friend.

'How, Chett,' he grinned through puffed lips. 'Nice timing.'

83

'How, Trav.' Allison nodded gravely. 'Let's go have a shot.'

'Guess I could use one at that.'

Nobody felt much like talking on the trail home except the kid. The left side of his jaw was badly swollen and discolored and his prominent eyes still appeared slightly out of focus. But it took more than that to keep Casey Stobaugh quiet, especially when he was mad clear through, white-hot mad and ranting.

'We could've finished him,' he said petulantly as the horses splashed noisily across a low stream. 'It was a fair fight. If someone gets killed in a fair fight, they let you off. Ain't that so, Wolf?'

'Huh? Oh, sure, kid, if you say so.'

Wolf had a loose tooth and a headache. But he was still looking better than new man Slattery, who'd been head-butted in the face. But this wasn't a sympathetic bunch, and certainly compassion played no part in Casey's response when his bleary gaze was drawn to the big guntipper.

His lip curled. 'How much are we forking out for this pistol-fighter, bro?' he demanded sarcastically. 'Whatever it is, it's too blamed much.'

'Easy,' Wolf said placatingly. 'None of us came out of that dust-up all that flash, Casey.'

'Gunfighters!' the boy snorted. He fingered his jaw and winced. 'Well, if these ripsnorters you've bought in can't do any better than the old bums we already got, maybe we'll have just face the fact that we gotta do something about Hightower's high-riders ourselves before they get made mayor or something. Did you hear those yellow-guts towners clapping? We're going to have to do something about some of those milquetoasts after we bury Hannibal, Wolf—'

'Forget the town,' Wolf cut in, granite jaw outthrust. 'But you're right about Allison and Traven, boy. Right now, let's just concentrate on them and how fine it'll be when we get square for today and every day.' He hipped around in his saddle and stared at each man in turn.

'You listening, boys?' he shouted, clenching a big fist. 'I want to see hate, and I want to feel it.'

Times like this Wolf Stobaugh could be inspirational. He'd hired new guns which he couldn't afford, and they'd had an almost victory snatched from their grasp on their first formal appearance on the streets. He had to bring them up out of that setback, and succeeded.

Suddenly everyone was responding, and Wolf saw in each face the slow simmering kind of rage that would go on cooking until Hightower's top guns were dead.

# CHAPTER 6

# THE CONSPIRATORS

Something unusual happened next morning at sunup.

Angelina Hannibal disappeared from the Hightower headquarters.

A subsequent search revealed that Allison's room was also empty.

Five miles to the east, the buckboard and matched pair rounded a bend in the trail that brought the green summit of Tramp Hill into sight.

'Not far now,' Angelina murmured, handling the team expertly as they passed beneath a leaning pine.

'Uh huh.'

Allison was drowsing a little in the pale sunlight. He wore no hat and looked different from the sober-suited gunman the county had grown familiar with. Faded Levi's and butternut shirt opened at the neck both looked and felt relaxing. No guns. But they weren't far away, having been stashed under the seat after he'd surprised them both by accepting Angelina's impulsive invitation to take a run out to Achilles Flat at first light.

He was only human even if some believed otherwise, he mused with a self-deprecating grin. He had no objections to going buggy-riding with a pretty woman even if by so doing he might well rile his employer. He'd expected it to be relaxing, yet was amazed at just how good it really felt. The sunshine, the lazy Sunday atmosphere, the absence however brief of the tension and danger that crowded his days. You couldn't buy this.

'Mind if I smoke?'

'Not at all.'

He drew a silver cigar case from his pants' pocket and set a stogie alight with a pocket flint. He caught her glancing at him sideways, half-smiled. 'Bad habit. Or at least, so they say.'

'There are worse habits.'

He wasn't about to go down that road. After a testy beginning he seemed to have struck up an easy friendship with Angelina Hannibal. They enjoyed talking books, people, theatres they might have both seen . . . cattle, horses and even politics. The girl had a wide range of knowledge of them all. But they steered clear of such contentious topics as range wars and the 'extreme lengths' people were often forced to go to in prosecuting them, such as hiring professional gunmen; or worse, he supposed, such as being such men. They cleared a belt of trees and the Achilles Flat spread lay before them across the stream, with Tramp Hill rising behind.

He'd been here only once before. Soon after his arrival he'd surveyed the spot where they'd murdered ramrod Chev Best, the incident that had transformed the long-running feud between Cross-T and Hightower into open war.

Angelina reined in and looped the reins around the brake with a deft movement. She wore gloves, plaid blouse and split riding skirt and boots. Her skin was smooth and fresh and today she looked more a woman than a girl. But still too young, he mused, and wondered what the hell he meant by that.

'Chev set up out here because he was planning to get married,' she said. 'This was to be his girl's surprise.' She smiled. 'I talked father into giving him the land. Of course, it's not that father's not generous, but the troubles have been costing so much that he really can't afford to be that way. No doubt about it. Running range wars is a good way to go bust. Everything costs, especially personnel.'

She glanced at him sharply.

'Father says you're worth every cent he pays you.'

He shrugged. Troubles seemed far away. Even yesterday's incident in Buffalo Gate was dim when viewed from this peaceful perspective.

'Why are we here?' he inquired.

She smiled, untied the ribbons and clicked the horses into a walk. 'I'll show you.' The house was small, solidly built and surrounded by a sturdy stake-and-ride fence. There was a woodpile, a couple of outbuildings, a front porch – and geese.

They came squawking up from the creek and

Angelina took a box from behind the seat and began moving about broadcasting dried corn pellets which the birds fought over clamorously.

'Chev brought them out here, and then within three months they were left to fend for themselves,' she said whimsically, brushing back a strand of fair hair. She paused, gazing up at the hill where the former ramrod had trailed his cow and the thief that fateful morning. 'I wonder . . . I wonder if this country will ever be different. . . ?'

'I like to think we can make it so.'

He wasn't avoiding contentious territory any longer. He sensed she wanted to talk openly at last, maybe had even brought him out here for that very purpose.

'You really believe in what you do, don't you?'

'I did.'

'Meaning you don't now?'

'What makes you ask that?'

'You do. Your eyes give you away at times. Such as directly after the battle at Tumbleweed Ridge. Ned was exultant but you were withdrawn for days afterwards. Isn't that so?'

He shrugged, strolling about amongst the satiated geese.

'Ned and I are different.'

'Totally so.'

'Why do you say that?'

'Well, I'm sure that would be obvious to a blind man. I almost like Ned, but he lives, eats and breathes trouble. He'd pick a fight with himself if there was nobody else around.'

He half-smiled. 'Yes, he's like that.'

'But you're not, are you, Chett? You'd give it all away if you could. I can tell.'

He halted with a frown, his grey eyes probing.

'You're leading up to something, Angelina. What is it?'

'You told me you feel indebted to Ned for saving your life. Well, by all accounts you just saved his in town. Doesn't that make you even?'

His face closed. Maybe she was right, he mused. She was certainly right about him being tired of the game. What Angelina didn't know was that, good pard that Trav might be, loyalty to him wasn't the only reason Chett Allison still hired his guns. He'd been at it so long, made so many enemies, that he wasn't sure any longer that he'd survive as a regular citizen if he ever hung up the Colts.

'Chett, I'm still curious about Ned.'

'I thought we'd done with that.'

'You . . . you didn't know he was coming to Hightower, did you?'

'Look, Angelina, I don't want—'

'You were shocked when you saw him here. I was there. I saw it. Tell me, why does he tag you around?'

He looked away. He could have evaded the issue but what was the point? For the truth was that he'd accepted Hannibal's job offer and had set out for Hightower without informing his sometime partner. But Traven had gotten wind of it somehow and beat him here. He knew why. Or at least he had a theory.

He stared across the rollicking creek.

'Ned's scared.'

She looked incredulous. 'That one scared? Of anything? I can't believe that.'

'Everyone's scared of something. I'm scared I've stayed in this business too long and might never be able to quit. Ned's scared because everybody hates him but me.'

'And that's the only reason you put up with him? Because he saved your life?'

He grinned.

'Not really. Ned's ten times a sonova, but we hit it off fine. I reckon that because he riles just about everyone he meets he's got this big fear that if I'm not around someday nobody'll want to give him the time of day. That he'd be nothing. So he figures if he tags after me, and keeps me alive, he might not just shrivel up and blow away on the next wind because nobody gives one sweet damn if he lives or dies.'

'That's terribly sad.'

'That's how it is though.'

'But you'd rather ride alone now.'

'Could be. Maybe I could ease out of the game gradually if I was working alone, take up storekeeping or whatever. But with Ned about I somehow feel I ought accept the next gun job – because he can't do anything else.' He shrugged. 'So it goes.'

'I see. So, you'll stay a gunfighter until they kill you?'

He looked up. Too nice a day to get burdened with such weighty matters. He grinned, stripping years from his face.

'Better be getting back. Some people might be still pretty sore about what happened yesterday.'

Angelina returned his smile.

'Surely this is an insult, Chett Allison? Are you saying you'd rather listen to father complaining about expenses, or looking for more fights you might get into, than spend time with a girl on such a pretty day?'

He just laughed and volunteered to drive back as they walked to the rig. But during the return journey his manner grew serious, his thoughts running deep. He kept glancing sideways at Angelina Hannibal, and was growing increasingly conscious that today, this Nevada Sunday, was slowly unfolding as one of the most significant days of his entire life.

Maybe it had been visiting that little spread, he mused. A simple man building something for a future that had nothing to do with guns and funerals. He kept catching fleeting images of Best working and planning and looking forward to tomorrow, something Chett Allison hadn't done for a long time.

But what was to be gained by thinking that way now?

Angelina reached out to touch his arm in order to draw his attention to the vista unfolding before them as the homestead valley opened up ahead.

He stared down at her hand and his lips compressed. Don't be a fool, Allison. What you're thinking is impossible and insane. You are feeling relaxed and easy and maybe vulnerable right now, but all that will most likely change just as soon as you get back. And it did.

But it wasn't news of more trouble that greeted him at the big house, rather something totally unexpected. Belden Harte had sent an emissary out during their absence with an invitation. Under Harte's chairmanship, Wolf Stobaugh wanted to hold an inter-ranch meeting to discuss a truce.

Cash Slattery's tongue probed at a loose tooth.

'Any word back yet?'

'Give it time,' growled Wolf Stobaugh, picking desultorily on a chicken bone. 'They ain't gonna make up their minds on the spot.'

'Just as damn well, I say.' Casey Stobaugh was battered and blue yet sounded as feisty and edgy as ever as he lit a smoke and spat a fragment of tobacco from his lower lip. 'Talk peace!' he snorted. 'I'd rather hang by the heels until hell freezes over than have those bastards believe even for a second that we're backing down.'

Everybody stared at the kid – his brother, Seneca McVey, Slattery and Mason. The five from the previous day's street brawl in town were all assembled beneath the smoke-darkened ceiling of the Cross-T homestead, even if a couple looked like they'd be better off travelling into Buffalo Gate to have the doctor check them over.

'This your idea, Wolf?' Seneca McVey asked after a silence. 'The meeting, I mean. It don't rightly sound like you.'

'Maybe not all mine.'

'You mean most of it was Harte's?' Casey put in sharply.

Wolf shifted uneasily. Both kinfolk and friends knew he was tight with the government man, but he had to be careful not to reveal too much.

Yet the truth of the matter was that the 'truce' idea was Harte's entirely. Of course his brother was on target – the idea didn't sound like him.

Stobaugh was rough, raw and elemental, and blasting his enemies and plotting and scheming to become one of the biggest cowmen in the territory were more his style. But Harte had brains.

Harte had been real sore about the ruckus in Buffalo Gate. Yet in a perplexing way he had reacted almost as though he was glad they'd clashed with Traven and Allison in front of the whole damn town.

'That ruckus made me take the blinkers off and see things as they really are, not how I want them to be,' Harte had told him during their high-tension meeting at the rep's office late last night.

'Which is?' Stobaugh had asked, puzzled.

'We're losing.'

'Judas, man, just on account we get into a bit of a brawl that goes against us—'

'That's part of it.' Harte began pacing up and down, a habit of his when tension was riding high. 'One man edges five. What do you make of that – partner?' He held up a hand; he didn't want an answer. 'What it means, is something none of us have wanted to admit since that pair showed up through the tall and uncut like the Sioux at Little Big Horn.'

'Which is?'

Harte faced him squarely.

'They've got our measure. Sure, they've got a lot of men riding behind them, and Hightower's taken on a new lease of life because of Allison and Traven. But

94

the simple truth is that that pair is out of our class, and what we have to do now is take some time out to regroup. We have to sit down calmly and plan out, first and foremost, just how to counter them before we go any further. They are the enemy now, not Hannibal. Allison and Traven first – worry about Hightower later. Time out for priorities, partner.'

'Take time out?' Wolf's jaw hung loose. 'You're talking hogswill, man. How can we? Hightower is in prime fighting trim, and what happened yesterday is only like to encourage them. You think they'll play along and just agree to sit back and jawbone if we ask it? That's loco! They'd come after us like they were starving and just heard the dinner gong.'

'How could they if we were all of us in the middle of a peace parley?'

'Huh?'

'We're going to convince Colonel Goddamn Hannibal that we have had enough and want to talk terms. We can lie, cheat, break into tears if that's what it takes to convince them we're genuine. We'll press for a cease-fire. When we get it we'll use the time to come up with the scheme that'll bring them down, otherwise we are in danger of losing the whole damn shebang. Do you understand me?'

Stobaugh hadn't really understood then.

But overnight with the help his best buddy, John Barleycorn, he'd made a calmer appraisal of the situation and realized his partner could be right.

Now he wanted the others to understand, particularly his inner circle. But that would take time. They all loved to fight, and yesterday had fired them up, even if they'd taken a whipping. But they were only eager to retaliate out of cussedness and vanity. Wolf Stobaugh felt as bad as they did but the difference was he was aiming for the brass ball in the golden circle; he was keeping his eye on the main game.

So Harte had to be right. A cease-fire. Then eliminate the fast guns first, Hightower next.

They all had another shot and were still arguing when hoofbeats sounded.

They tiled out into the yard as young Tommy Marsh rode in and reined up. 'Hightower's agreed, Wolf,' the rider grinned. 'Said they'll be at the council chambers at noon.' He sobered. 'That guy Traven, though. He said to tell you if this is some kind of trick he'll personally blast you all then sell your women to cathouses in Utah.'

The young man flushed. 'Told me to make sure I said it just like that or he'd . . . well, I don't wanna repeat all he said—'

'That dirty-mouthed sonofa—' Casey Stobaugh hissed, but his brother signalled for silence.

'Thanks, Tommy,' Wolf said calmly. 'Now get back to town and tell Mr Harte we're with him all the way about the cease-fire.' He shot his scowling party an imperious look. 'And tell him it was unanimous. He's gonna be mighty glad to hear this, mighty glad, as he thought the boys here might be against it for some reason.'

Casey Stobaugh cursed but didn't take it further. When the chips were down, he always knuckled under to Wolf. They all did.

# CHAPTER 7

# WHEN NOMAD
# CAME BACK

Quint Nomad was finally leaving the Indian country behind and heading north. He rode an Apache appaloosa with a black uncut mane and tail. The man was burned brown as an Indian by the south-western sun and smiled lazily as he covered the long horse miles. But with shoulder-length white hair and eyes of a singular piercing blue, he would never be mistaken for any breed of redskin, even if Indians might be about his favourite people right now.

The Apaches had taken him in the day he came crawling out of an Arizona dust storm more dead than alive with nothing but his sixshooters and a doeskin purse filled with golden coins.

He didn't have the coins any longer but the Apaches had given him something of infinite greater value in return. His life.

He'd been five days dying in the desert and damn near dead that day almost half a year ago when a squaw out hunting for prairie dogs discovered him just half a mile from the stronghold, yet despite an iron will and a once-powerful body he was unable to crawl another inch.

Now he rode arrow straight through a vast and dreamlike country towards the 'sharp end' of Nevada's southeastern corner where the mighty Colorado River jigsawed its way through its awesome stone canyons to form the border with Arizona.

A promise to a man like this meant something very different from what it meant to most men. For Quint Nomad it meant a return to the land and the life he'd had to surrender in agony months before. It also meant that his very first step upon reaching the Goldfield region, would be to stop by at a grimed and gritty prairie noplace named Pioche Butte which he couldn't think of without reviving memories of the pain he'd been in when he'd staggered into that pest hole in late summer.

They could say what they liked about childbirth pain and Injun tortures but he believed what he'd endured that day to be as bad as a man could ever endure.

He was packing three bullets in his body when he rode into Pioche Butte. They were inside him after they'd robbed him and kicked him out again, more dead than alive. Yet he grinned now, as with the Colorado well behind him, he soaked up the familiar Nevadan landscapes, the alkali sinks and great arid stretches clothed in sagebrush and creosote bush. In the distance was one of the mountain chains which generally ran north and south, segmenting the wide land. He was heading for the high plateau areas that were so good for grazing, and so attracted settlement, pioneers and men like Quint Nomad. Indians were thin on the ground in this quarter of the state but luckily that had not been the case down in Arizona where he'd somehow managed to wander in a blanked-out daze of pain fever.

Luckily for him the Apaches had proven more hospitable than his white brothers, not only expertly prizing the lead out of him but nursing him back to full strength, and eventually beyond that point. Far beyond.

The latter part of his convalescence had seen the gunman – some said the top gun of them all – achieve something remarkable, transcending even his former high levels of physical and mental powers by doing what he thought of now as 'going Injun.'

His close brush with death and a full awareness of what he intended doing once he quit the Indian country and returned to 'civilization', had combined to help him stage his remarkable recovery. It was then that he became exposed to something on the Arizona plains which suggested he might go even further, reach higher.

The Apaches, still warlike and fighting the Bluecoats and settlers on several fronts, trained their young in the warrior's art. In winter the youths were dropped in freezing lakes and rivers and were often left swimming there until they had to be fished out, sometimes apparently more dead than alive. But they were alive, and next day they would be back in the river, each boy intent on surviving longer, driving their bodies to the limits and beyond.

On a raging summer's day a boy would be given an amount of water to hold in his mouth, then sent off to climb a mountain and return at dusk. If, when he spat out, there was anything less than the cup of water, he would do the marathon again. It was cruel and brutal, but what warriors were made!

Nomad had lost count of the freezing swims and scorching mountain runs he'd voluntarily accomplished under the watchful eyes of the tribal elders over the long weeks. But now he carried the benefits of his Spartan programme in his body and mind on this journey, as he hummed an Indian song in the chilling twilight.

A mile further on, he crossed a dried-out creekbed and jerked the horse right as he kneed it up a long red slope which led to the outlaw trail and a place called Pioche Butte below Crimson Rose Mesa.

He inhaled powerfully. His body was iron, his stamina without limit. And most important of all, his super fitness had seen him improve upon his already matchless speed with the Colts.

Many experts had already rated Quint Nomad the best before his almost fatal gunfight. Now, following his months of preparation for his comeback, he finally agreed. He was the best, the nonpareil.

But what was the point of honing and enhancing a great natural skill if a man didn't put it to practical purpose?

A wolf smile creased his face at that thought. Yet

the strange thing was that he felt far less bitter towards the man who'd shot him in a fair fight, than those who had treated him with such viciousness after the event.

But both would pay, in time.

Nightfall found him sitting on his horse and gazing down on a frail ring of lights far out on the face of the darkening plain that marked the location of a human hell hole called Pioche Butte. His vantage point was the hump-backed Crimson Rose Mesa – named after some forgotten loser's lost love, or so he'd been told.

The last time he'd ridden through the shadows of the Crimson Rose he was packing three bullets in his body and reckoned he wouldn't last twenty-four hours' life ahead if he didn't get help, fast.

The sun-bleached falsefronts of the ugliest town he'd ever seen had looked like a beacon of hope that bloody day.

Absently fingering one of the scars he'd been left with after an Apache medicine man hacked three .45 slugs from chest, groin and thigh, he pushed the weary pony downslope and headed for the lights, and the tune he was whistling was 'Johnny In The Cold Ground.'

Pioche Butte town hadn't changed. No reason it should. It had been a scum-hole then, still was. A derelict staggered across his path as his horse stirred up the deep dust of the single street, and it could have been the self-same man who'd helped him down out of his saddle the night he rode in more dead than alive.

Music drifted from a converted horse barn with the word 'Liquor' daubed across its scabrous front wall in whitewashed letters five feet tall.

He felt a tingle in his wrists as he inhaled the evil night humours and guided his horse to the collapsing tie-rail, bringing it in neat.

A gust of dust wind seemed to boost him through plank doors that were tied back in silent invitation to welcome the weary traveller. He knew if he looked closely enough he would find his own bloodstains on those doors from his prior visit. He'd been leaking blood on his way into Liquor that night and considerably more when he left. He savoured his moment before stepping in beneath the harsh glare of twin kerosene lamps hanging from an invisible ceiling, and he took a deep breath when he saw them holding court at the high end of the uneven plank bar, exactly as had been the case almost half a year ago.

Jellison and Crowe, mayor and saloonkeeper of Pioche Butte respectively. Yessir! Exactly as it had been.

Nomad halted and stood motionless.

One by one the slatternly women, ruined men, scrawny kids and all the other losers and tattered bums grew aware of this upright, stalwart figure with the shoulder length hair and glittering blue eyes. He waited for recognition to strike, forgetting for the moment that this stalwart specimen in the fringed buckskin jacket which he was presenting before them surely in no way could resemble that gun-shot wreck who'd staggered in here that night nineteen weeks ago.

'What?'

It was Mayor Jellison who finally eased his bulging backside round on his outsized stool to realize something unusual was happening.

Then, 'Who be you?' saloonkeeper Crowe demanded suspiciously. 'What do you want?'

Nomad smiled. 'My blood's on your doors – scum.'

What kind of introduction was this?

The two took another long hard look at the 'stranger', then at one another. A snap of Jellison's fat fingers brought two husky men around from behind the bar, scowling and ready for action.

'Wiseacres not welcome,' Jellison rumbled. 'OK, boys.'

The bruisers started forward, stopped on a dime. They were staring at twin revolvers which seemed to have filled the stranger's hands by sleight-of-hand.

'What—?' Crowe began, but the stranger had the floor.

'Nomad's the name, gents. You'd remember it from the billfold you stole the night I came in here all shot to hell and you robbed me and beat up on me then threw me out into the street to die.' A telling pause. Then, softly, 'But I didn't, as you can see.'

Crowe actually shrieked like a woman as recognition hit. The sound of that terrified cry sent a thrill of pure pleasure coursing through the gunfighter's body. Emotionlessly, outwardly calm, Nomad cut loose. His bullets caught Crowe square in the face with such force that his body was belted halfway across the bartop before slumping and subsiding there like a sack of bloody meat.

The sounds of pure terror that erupted threatened to drown out the deep-throated roar of the big revolvers. But in the end the guns prevailed and four men lay dead under the harsh lights, the ears of the living so dulled and deafened by the sixgun cacophony that they could still barely hear a full minute later when the hoofbeats of the Indian pony rose outside then quickly faded into the night.

Two days later Quint Nomad rode into a gritty railroad town where his first stopover was the bathhouse where he treated himself to a 'civilized' soaking for the first time in half a year, a luxury that used up most of the last coins he had left.

Sunk up to his hard jaws in frothy suds, he scanned the local paper leisurely. Some time later, he turned a page and was confronted by a glaring headline:

## CHETT ALLISON RIDES HIGH IN VULCAN COUNTY!

With a curious, almost sickening surge of excitement, the gunfighter read and re-read the report on the Vulcan County range war, until he almost knew it by heart.

As he whispered the words, he was unaware that beneath the froth and bubbles he was fingering the brutal scars in chest, groin and thigh. Scars from the three bullets Chett Allison had pumped into him the night he left him for dead.

December was turning the valleys gold as Allison and

Traven rode the river trail from Hightower to Buffalo Gate. There was a bite in the wind that warned of colder weather on the way. Despite the frosts, both banks of the river were still fringed with green laguna and today there was sunlight dappling through gaunt willows.

The men rode side by side, Allison astride his ugly grulla with the uneven gait, Traven on his husky big black with the silver worked harness. Allison wore his regular dark suit while his partner sported a garishly-checked shirt opened halfway to the waist in defiance of the cold.

Allison tugged a gold watch from his pocket, consulted it and replaced it in silence. Traven cocked an eyebrow at him. 'That's about the third time you've looked at that thing since we quit the spread. What's the matter – nervous?'

'Could be.'

Traven caught the glint of humour in his eyes, but his powerful scarred face remained sober.

'Then let's drop this crackbrained notion of a peace parley with Cross-T and get on back to the spread. Or better still, let's go to town anyway and hit the saloons. I got me a big fat blonde at the Queen who ain't sighted me in way too long.'

Allison tilted his hat forward a little. 'No, they asked for a parley. It won't hurt to see what they've got in mind.'

'What if it's some kind of trap, goddamnit?'

'Nervous?'

Traven chuckled now. 'Knew you'd get back at me. But no, to tell the truth I don't believe they'd have the guts to try anything in town in broad daylight, especially with the government rep in the chair. What's that stuffed shirt's handle again?'

'Harte – Belden Harte.'

'Yeah, Harte. Well, I suppose it'd have to be odds against a joker like that having a hand in anything dicey.' He paused to spit into the brush. 'But what the hell's it gonna achieve? In the month we've been riding for the colonel we've seen enough of Cross-T to know they're no bunch of schoolma'ams. They've given as good as they've got and have thrown up enough lead to gum up the river, so what would they want a peace treaty for?'

'Maybe Stobaugh's had enough. A man can get sick of killing, Ned.'

Traven's stare was probing but Allison's face was blank. A half-mile passed in silence. Traven lit a black cigar, drew on it forcefully and exhaled a gust of smoke that was swept away by the wind.

'You getting tired of the game, Chett?'

'It's my living.'

'That don't answer me.'

'Well, no, I guess it doesn't. But if you want to know the truth, I think it was a pretty damn-fool question, Ned.'

Traven shrugged. 'Just curious.'

'Why'd you ask?'

'Damnit, Chett, I tell you I was just jawing.'

'You think I'm going soft?'

'Chett Allison going soft? Crazy.' He shifted his weight in the saddle and the black grunted. 'No, it's just that I've had the notion that your mind wasn't right on the job.'

'Well, the job's going right, isn't it? We've been knocking Stobaugh's backside loose ever since we signed on, haven't we?'

'Sure. It's just that you don't seem to have the interest, that maybe you got something on your mind. Look, there's no call for us to argue, man. I always talk too damn much, you know that better than anybody.'

There was silence for a time as they rounded a wide bend in the river, and Traven thought the discussion was over until Allison spoke quietly, soberly: 'It's got to end one day, man.'

Traven felt a sudden chill. 'What has?'

Allison made a sweeping gesture with his left hand. 'All of it – this whole crazy business.'

'Bushwa! There'll be work for trigger-happy pilgrims like us for as long as the West is greedy and gutless and full of hate, and I calculate that'll be for all time.'

'I don't mean that. I mean it'll end for you and me. How many times have you been shot, Ned?'

'I don't see what the hell that has—'

'How many?'

'All right – eight.'

'Eight . . . and you're still breathing.'

'Call me lucky,' Traven said cynically.

'Sure, sure. Well, I've stopped serious lead four times myself. But a man's luck has to run out some day. What then?'

'This don't sound like you, Chett. Damnation, you know this is the only life. It's the danger that gives it the tang, keeps you young, hungry to freakin' live. Can you imagine hanging up the Colts and sitting back and getting fat and contented on a spread with a rocker on the porch knowing that in ten years' time you'd still be likely there, still rocking and growing fatter by the day?' When Allison made no immediate reply, he added with a hint of anxiety, 'Well, can you?'

Allison's reply was barely audible. 'Maybe I can.'

At that moment a pair of longspurs arrowed up almost from under Traven's mount. The black side-stepped in fright and was quickly brought under control.

The incident served as a punctuation in a conversation, which for some reason now Traven no longer wished to continue. For it had been leading into an area he always strove to avoid, namely the possibility that Allison might one day quit the life, either from weariness and dissatisfaction – or maybe because of someone.

He thought briefly of Angelina Hannibal, recalling the way she watched Allison when she thought nobody noticed. He pictured the couple strolling about the headquarters yard on dusk most days, acting like they had known one another for years.

That girl hated gunfighters and had made it plain. Even more obvious was the fact that, somewhere along the way, she'd made Allison the exception to that rule.

He shook his head angrily and lit a fresh stogie. Chett would never quit the game. He was like himself – had it in his blood.

They rode on in silence towards Buffalo Gate.

\*

The chief marshal slung the pink telegraph slip across his littered desk. 'Read that.'

His bearded visitor seated opposite was a military adviser to the governor. He was also one of the marshal's more reliable associates in this inconspicuous grey building situated on a quiet back street half a mile from the state house; a jumbled maze of offices, corridors, staff rooms and living quarters.

The real power was exercised at the state house, but officials like the chief marshal's friend also had considerable authority. They wielded this quietly and effectively, far from the glare of publicity, which mostly focused upon the government of the day in any case.

The officer scanned the wire, sat down and leaned back.

'Harte's taking a new tack down there, it would seem. Conferences now.' He lifted grizzled brows. 'Think that might work?'

'Well, Hightower's agreed to at least talk. That has to be some sort of step in the right direction.'

The adviser glanced at the wall clock.

'If nothing goes wrong in the meantime they'll be meeting about now.' He frowned, something he often did when discussing Vulcan County. 'Harte's got Stobaugh thinking his way, it would seem, which is no mean effort. And with Allison representing Hightower, that has to be a plus.'

'Ahh, Jake,' the marshal sighed, stretching long arms at the ceiling, 'just listen to us, will you? Here we are; we've got a gunfighter playing a key role in a conference that could mean the difference between peace and chaos in the provinces, and we're actually pleased to hear it. Is this progress or is it hypocrisy?'

'Expediency. That's what it is.'

'Explain.'

'I've been here longer than you, Marshal. I was here in 1864 when President Lincoln signed the proclamation of statehood for this territory even though we did not actually meet the population requirement for this elevation in status.'

'So?'

'So, underpopulation of such a large region was the problem then, and still is. In particular this affects government instrumentalities which have to cope with undermanning in virtually all areas of its jurisdiction. This is particularly worrisome in the disciplines such as law and order and distribution of military forces. There's never enough to go round. That's why in Vulcan County, as in many other quarters, when trouble erupts the government finds it lacks the resources to take the appropriate steps. Instead we all too often have to just sit back and hope things will settle of their own accord, as indeed they so often do, as you would know.'

The marshal nodded soberly.

He was new to the posting and chafed at what he regarded as the rule of gun law in several regions of the State of Nevada. But he was also a realist.

'Guess you're right, Jake. Still doesn't feel right, though.'

'When you're running an overtaxed administration you have to make the best of what you've got, Marshal.' The officer paused. 'But offhand I'd suggest we couldn't have anyone more suited to the task than Allison. He's a gunman, sure. But he has an impressive record as a peacemaker and enforcer and seems to have a talent for aligning himself with what we here regard as the good guys in these ugly range wars, mining disputes and suchlike.' He nodded. 'Uh huh, I'll go on record as saying that if Harte can hammer out some sort of armistice in that mess down there, we'll find it was largely due to Allison's involvement.'

'He's not alone, you know?'

The adviser nodded soberly. 'I know. Traven. Still, my instincts tell me that Allison might still be able to swing it. If we could just secure an armistice for a few weeks we might be in a position by then to dispatch a cavalry unit down there and screw down the lid on their troubles.'

The chief marshal rose and took his favourite pipe from a desk rack. He smoked ever increasingly these days as he hunted down outlaw gangs more and dealt with troublemakers on the streets of the capital less. He was an outdoors man and could fully appreciate the sweeping scale of the troubles in the plateau country.

'Well, much obliged, Jake. You've notched up my optimism some even if it's still not sky high. I'd offer you a drink but I quit drinking in office hours ever since those hours got to be twelve or fourteen long. Maybe tomorrow?'

The adviser smiled and made for the door.

'Hopefully by tomorrow we'll have word that Harte's meeting has been a success.'

'I'd like to believe that.' The chief marshal stood at a window staring down into the parade ground where junior cavalrymen in butternut grey were going through arms drill. 'Just as I'd like to believe Harte is up to the job we gave him.' He frowned hard. 'You know, it seems to me there's something going on with our Vulcan rep that I just can't put a finger on, lately.'

'I'd best leave before you start having doubts about me, Marshal,' the adviser smiled easily, and left.

'No, not you, Jake,' the marshal murmured as he fingered fresh shag cut into his pipe. 'Just Belden Harte . . . .' He gave an impatient grunt, put the pipe away unlit and went to his liquor cabinet to break his own ban against working-hours drinking. When a man began harbouring doubts about long serving officers with immaculate records, and fretting about gunslingers acting as a substitute for law and order, whiskey plainly was no longer an indulgence but a necessity.

Coincidentally, at almost the same moment a hundred miles away, the man the chief marshal was frowning about, was himself leaning back in a padded chair at the head of a long table in the conference room of the Buffalo Gate City Council chambers, waiting for the swallow of rye he'd just taken to hit his gut.

At the far end of the table, Wolf Stobaugh was the

sole remaining conference guest.

It had been a disaster, which a brooding Harte believed might well have been avoided but for the lacerating presence of Stobaugh junior. That kid just never shut up. And after Traven threatened to take his pants down and paddle his backside, no amount of gavel-banging by the self-elected chairman could salvage the situation.

Despite the fact that genuine peace was the last thing the conspirators wanted they were peeved that their hastily contrived scheme to buy breathing space had failed so dismally.

The way people had stomped out of this room, they'd be lucky if this phony 'peace' lasted even forty-eight hours.

'What now?' Wolf rumbled at length.

Harte's sigh was windy.

'Better prepare to defend, I guess.'

'I'm better at attack.'

'Attack . . . defend, who gives a damn.' Harte was down but knew he'd bounce back. What he couldn't know was that the decision on if and when the war might resume was no longer his to make.

# CHAPTER 8

# ROUGH COMPANY

'Ahh, good sports with ready cash,' the gambler greeted, flashing a gold-toothed smile. 'Just the gentlemen I've been looking for. How's about getting together and making up a little game and—'

'Why don't you take your lousy game and plug it, Duggan!' Casey Stobaugh snarled, glaring up from his drink.

The gambler's professional grin faded. He glanced questioningly at Casey, then at his companions, McVey, Cormorant and Judd Smith. Smith shook his bullet head warningly and the player wandered away to be lost in the noisy crowd filling the Silver Dollar Saloon.

'The man never meant no harm, Casey,' McVey said placatingly. The Arizonan gunpacker's hawk face was marked by fading bruising now yellowing at the edges, testimony of recent violence.

'The hell with him,' Casey retorted sulkily. He

took another pull on his glass, belched and stared at each man in turn. 'The hell with everybody – Wolf, Harte – everybody.'

'Still sore, kid?' Cormorant queried. Like Stobaugh, the gunman was showing signs of the liquor they'd been putting away over the past few hours. Not drunk yet, but not sober, either.

'Well, ain't you?' the youngster challenged. He made a chopping motion with his right hand. 'They walked all over you in that stinking meeting too, as I recall. But I sure don't recollect you sassing Traven any when we came out.'

Cormorant looked uneasy. 'Hell, Casey, who wants to fuss with that one if he don't have to? Besides, we was under orders not to start anything, if you recall. Wolf said so.'

'Ah, stow it!' Casey snapped.

Now Cormorant fell silent, as did the others. From experience they knew better than to cross the kid when he was in one of his rages. They were in no way afraid of him, but could never forget he was Wolf's brother.

Nobody wanted to risk getting on Wolf's bad side. Ever.

Even so they often found the kid's tantrums and violent outbursts hard to take, even if tonight there was some sympathy for the way he was acting up.

For all had been present at the council chambers meeting, all had smarted under Allison's arrogance and Traven's sneering offensiveness when things began to come apart. Sure, maybe Wolf and Casey had doomed the whole thing to failure with their demands and their cussedness, yet the gunmen still laid the blame for the breakdown at the feet of the Hightower's guns.

It seemed in retrospect that Traven had arrived at the meeting with the intention of scuttling it. Several times Allison had rebuked his gun *segundo*. But when the Stobaughs began retaliating and making demands which they were certain would never be met, it became an inevitable case of 'last out douse the lights'.

They still didn't understand what had prompted Harte to proffer the olive branch in the first place, although Wolf had let something slip the previous day about the need of a breathing space.

But win, lose or draw, the visit to town was a first-rate excuse to tie one on, and the trio had managed to get Casey Stobaugh calmed down some by around eight when two things occurred to change the tempo of the night. The saloon's new singer came on stage to belt out a bracket of well-received songs, and the louvred doors swung open to admit Chett Allison and Ned Traven.

Facing the doors, Judd Smith swallowed his liquor too fast and began to cough.

'What's the matter with you?' Casey demanded irritably, before growing aware of the turning heads. He glanced into the big mirror and spotted the new arrivals. Slowly and deliberately, he lowered his glass to the zinc-top bar. His knuckles were white. Studying him closely, Seneca McVey said quietly, 'Mebbe it's time we headed back for the spread, Casey boy.'

'What's the matter, McVey? They got you that

jittery you don't feel up to even staying in the same room? The hell! We were here first. If anybody feels they gotta move on, they can.'

'They're coming over,' Drum Cormorant said uneasily.

'Now take it easy, kid,' McVey warned softly.

Casey's mumbled response was unintelligible. But there was no misreading the hot flush diffusing his face as he stared unblinking into the mirror to watch the two approach.

McVey was not alone in advocating calm; Chett Allison was doing the self-same thing as drinkers gave way before them, opening up a path to the bar.

'Just let me do the talking, Trav. We all had our wrangle at the chambers and it finished there. *Sabe?*'

'Hell, all I want is a long cold one, and I sure ain't interested in a bunch of tenth-raters and a runny-nosed kid. I'll order a couple while you ask after the big feller.'

'Good idea.'

'Allison,' rugged Smith said guardedly, moving a little away from the bar. It was growing very quiet apart from the sound of the piano. No sign of the new songbird now. Maybe she'd worked saloons before and had developed a sixth sense that warned her when there was a change of atmosphere.

'Is Wolf still in town?' Allison inquired.

Smith jerked his thumb. 'Gone back to the spread.'

'Too bad. Wanted to talk to him.'

'Hey, wake up, barslop!' Traven said loudly from farther along the bar. 'Two beers – and pronto!'

117

Allison started in his direction, but suddenly Casey Stobaugh moved to block his path.

'What do you want with my brother, Allison?'

Chett flicked grey eyes at him. 'Nothing that can't wait.' Without adding anything, he stepped round the man and reached for the beer Traven proffered.

There was a crash as Stobaugh's flung glass hit the floor and shattered.

'I asked you a straight question, mister!' he ranted. 'What do you want with Wolf, damn you?'

It had been quiet before; now it was totally silent. Every eye in the smoky room focused on the tall figure of the gunfighter as he lowered his glass and glanced sideways at Traven. Then they saw Seneca McVey take Casey by the elbow and whisper fiercely to him as his fingers dug deep. For a moment Casey appeared to listen. Then suddenly he cursed, shook loose and moved to lean his back against the bar to glare venomously at Allison. He was cursing.

Chett didn't raise his voice. 'You've had a few, Stobaugh. Might be an idea if you headed for home and had a talk with your brother. He'd likely agree with me that—'

'The hell I will!'

Casey Stobaugh was in the grip of something bigger than himself as he thrust a nervous Cormorant out of his way and stood facing the two gunfighters squarely, jaw jutting, bristling like a bantam cock.

'You don't scare me one lick, Allison. And no cheap gunslick tells me what to do – no way!' His eyes were bugging and his hands shook like a man gripped by anger or fear, it was hard to tell which. But it was plain he'd isolated himself, and despite his fury, he backed up a step as Allison moved up on him.

Chett's face looked drawn and tight.

'All right, boy – brat, whatever you are. I'm looking for your brother to talk over what happened earlier. To see if maybe just the two of us might sit down over a quiet drink and see if we can salvage something, before we start in shooting at one another again. But you don't want that, do you? You're one of the dumb ones who just want to rip and tear until you run out of luck and end up in a casket. That's not gutsy, Stobaugh, it's just plain dumb—'

'Ain't you heard, pard?' Traven growled from the bar. 'They call him the Dumbstruck Kid. Half-weaned and halfway to hell. That's where he'll stay until he starts learning to act like a grown-up.' He gestured impatiently. 'Leave him be. We can ride out and parley with the big fella in the morning if you want. Come on. And you sit down and shut up, kid.'

'OK, that'll do it, Trav,' Allison chided as he turned his back on the bar and moved away.

All eyes followed his tall figure, and there was an audible sigh of relief. They thought it was over. Only Traven it seemed caught the kill-crazy glitter that filled the drunken boy's eyes. With Allison between him and Stobaugh, he couldn't do anything but shout, 'Chett! Watch him!'

On the cry, Chett Allison spun and instinctively whipped out his right-hand Colt. His eyes snapped wide when he realized Stobaugh had cleared his pistol, saw his finger whitening as he applied first pressure to the trigger.

Chett's Colt belched flame and thunder.

There was a sharp metallic clash of sound as Stobaugh was engulfed in gunsmoke for a moment, and they saw his gun spin high into the air. Then with a ghastly, gagging grin, the young man reeled away, turning and twisting drunkenly until he crashed into a row of tables which collapsed beneath his weight.

Allison stood as though petrified, watching Stobaugh slide limply backwards to the floor. The slim body arched in agony until only head and heels touched the floor. He maintained the grotesque arch for an endless moment before his whole body went limp and didn't move again.

In the breathless moment that followed, Traven's twin revolvers jumped clear to cover the Cross-T gunmen. But the precaution wasn't necessary. Like everybody else, McVey's men were just staring from the body to Allison then back to the body again. Allison turned to the sea of faces, and his face was deeply pitted as if he was afflicted by the smallpox.

'I shot his gun,' he gasped. 'I didn't mean to kill—'

A man stooped and picked up Stobaugh's weapon from the floor fifteen feet along the bar. He held it up. The chamber was hanging half-out of its housing, and as the man touched it, bullets fell to the floor with a great clatter. The man stared around in astonishment. 'He aimed for the gun and . . . and he hit it. Dead centre. Only thing, the slug ricocheted the wrong way . . . .'

Traven cocked a gun hammer with a loud click.

'Get shook of them hoglegs right now.' His voice was flat and hard. The trio gaped at him then unbuckled their gunbelts and let them slide to the floor. Only then did Traven cross to Allison's side and take him by the arm. 'C'mon, Chett, let's go home.'

'Better get the sheriff . . .' Allison seemed dazed. 'I didn't try to kill him, Trav. He was just a kid . . . .'

'A loud-mouthed kid. Come on, we're going.'

It was a strange spectacle, Chett Allison allowing himself to be guided from the Yellow Dollar like a man in a trance. Traven, by contrast, was alert and watchful at his side, black eyes cutting this way and that for the first sign of danger. He had one hand on Allison's shoulder, the other clutching a Frontiersman model Colt.45, on full cock. But nobody impeded their exit, and even after they had gone, the crowd still seemed phase-locked by shock. There were two Hightower riders in the crowd, one of them an old, sharp-eyed horse-breaker who had once worn the guns himself, a man who understood what made a man like Chett Allison what he was.

The man stared at the doors for a long minute before turning to his partner.

'He made a mistake,' he said sympathetically. 'God help him, he made a mistake.'

Few men of the gun get to reach old age. In time, the life they follow strikes back. The human soul, no matter how brutalized by habit and custom, sickens of the killing. Something in the inner ear reacts badly when a gunfighter hears one death rattle too many, and the germ of death infects the deliverer of death himself.

Some are taken by melancholy and drink. Others simply grow more reckless and careless and run risks they would have once avoided. Unwittingly perhaps, they are courting death, while others begin thinking about retirement and anonymity away from the lethal streets.

Whichever way they respond, the outcome is rarely successful. A growing antipathy for the most lethal of all professions can lead to a falling off in the necessary skills a killer requires just to stay alive. . . .

The killing of Casey Stobaugh at the Yellow Dollar Saloon hit Chett Allison harder than anything in his career. The fact that the incident had been accidental, and was perceived to be that way, seemed to satisfy most people with a few notable exceptions. But he was not satisfied.

The spectacle of the man lying dead on the saloon floor was something he didn't seem able to shake from his thoughts. He slept badly, knew he was withdrawn and curt, avoided Angelina when he shouldn't have done, cut loose on Traven on occasion – but didn't drink.

Self-preservation warned that if he tried to drown this one in booze – in the middle of a range war – it could easily cost him his life.

And the war did resume.

Casey Stobaugh was barely cold in his grave before the Cross-T, personally led by Wolf Stobaugh, unleashed itself on Hightower in a series of raids which continued day and night and saw the casualty list on Hightower lengthen alarmingly despite a spirited defence.

Allison and Traven rode almost constantly – the very thing Chett didn't wish to do, but knew he must. It kept him from brooding. And the first raider he gunned after Casey Stobaugh didn't seem to mean a thing. They were the enemy, he the protector. As long as he felt that way he could continue to fight.

Colonel Hannibal, despite having been won over to Allison during the dangerous weeks the two had been riding for his brand, reacted badly to both Stobaugh's killing and the resulting upsurge in hostilities.

The man lapsed in moody silence when Allison was around and largely kept his own counsel. Occasionally he dashed off a stiff letter to the capital demanding assistance before total anarchy took over. The government's replies were polite and sympathetic, but the result was always the same. They were unable to help; they wished the colonel success.

So it went on and Vulcan County seemed to grow almost indifferent to it all, even the steady procession of journeys Esaw Mulligan's glossy black hearse made from his undertaking parlour to the cemetery beyond the town limits failing to rouse any real reaction.

For Angelina, the worsening in the shooting war was not her greatest concern. It was Allison that worried her most. But it was an ill wind that didn't blow somebody some good. In her case, she saw more of the gunfighter now than had been the case before, as she did what she could to drag him out of the pit he seemed to have slipped into following the incident at the Yellow Dollar.

In so doing, she fell in love.

This shocked her. At first. But there could be no denying the way her heart leapt whenever she saw him, how he was rarely out of her thoughts. Her revulsion for violent men had come full circle. She had fallen in love with a man who plainly had no room in his life for romance or anything like. A killer, if she would. But it still didn't change her feelings; she sometimes felt she loved him all the more, knowing it to be hopeless.

On the surface Traven seemed unaffected by the whole affair. He laughed, joked, insulted, brawled and fought like a tiger in the hills and valleys, just like before. Underneath there was a different Ned Traven.

He was a man designed by nature to alienate and be alienated. He possessed enough talents to qualify him for the role of gun hero most anyplace, but his personality was a guarantee against his ever being admired by anybody.

He made enemies as naturally as he breathed. They stretched back through his life, and he might well have been worn down and defeated by all this enmity he so naturally engendered, but for Allison.

Allison regarded him as his friend, which to Traven was interpreted as proof that he was something better than the alien scum most saw him to be.

Consequently, Traven had become Allison's watchdog, defender and champion, a role he'd mapped out for himself and which he discharged with a ruthless loyalty which he sometimes overplayed, for he was excessive by nature.

It was one early evening on Hightower, with a wintry sunset fading away in the west and the howls of a man being operated upon to remove a Cross-T slug from his guts grating on the nerve-ends of a bunch of weary hands waiting for chow, that an outspoken newcomer named Rip Stang, weary and red-eyed, just had to grouse.

'Just goes on and on,' he growled. 'I've lost count the number of boys who've stopped lead here over the last two weeks. And all because of him.'

'Who?' a narrow-faced waddy demanded.

'Mr High-and-mighty,' Stang said. 'Allison. If he hadn't got to showing off and taken that pot-shot at Casey Stobaugh, the war would have just gone on slow and easy like always. Who knows? This circus might have even been all over by this.'

Reactions were guarded.

A few had been critical over the Stobaugh incident, but most understood its inevitability. But pro or con, it wasn't something men fretted about to any degree now. Some glanced around nervously to make certain the new man's remarks weren't over-heard. Allison was touchy on the Stobaugh subject, Traven likewise.

But one fellow nursing a slinged arm, grunted a response that sounded something like agreement, and that was all Stang needed to continue.

'From what I've seen of this Allison,' he stated righteously, 'it's him who runs this whole she-bang, not Hannibal.'

'Well,' a man argued, 'he's a gunfighter, ain't he?'

Stang gave the man a hard stare. 'And what am I, and Taller and Kells? We're all gunfighters but we don't act like we're God Almighty. All we do is take orders and get shot at.'

'Well, you can't say Chett don't know his business.'

'Would any jasper who knew his business have had that run-in with Cross-T just when things were looking promising? Killed the dopey kid? That's why we're ducking lead twenty-four hours a day now, you know. Allison's mistake. If you ask me it's time some of us foot soldiers got together and had a say in how things are run around here. Could be high time Allison stopped playing God and passed the reins over to someone who can end this war instead of just making it worse.'

Traven came out of the deepening gloom along the side of the cookhouse so swiftly and silently he was in their midst before they realized it. His right arm was heavily bandaged following a fall from his horse during a skirmish at Spider Seep. He came to a sudden halt with hands on hips, black eyes murderous as he glared at Stang.

The men edged away, but the new hand faced him defiantly.

A sneer rode Traven's mouth. 'You know, I've been waiting to hear somebody sing that song, Stang.'

'It's nothing but the truth, Traven.'

'Is that so? You were bad-mouthing a pard of mine. You who are nothing but a plaster-gutted, hollowed-out son of a yellow dog bitch!'

'I got a right to my say.'

'And I've got a right to this!'

With the word, Traven punched the man hard in the mouth. He kicked him in the crotch and he doubled over with a scream. The sound seemed to inflame Traven the more. With enormous power, he seized Stang in a wrestling grip, dragged him across to the trough and forced his face close to the water.

'You need your mouthed washed out, scum!' he panted, and shoved his head under. The hands watched in anxious silence, alarmed if scarcely surprised. Some figured Stang had it coming. All expected Traven would make his point then let him up. This didn't happen. The seconds ticked by and Stang's struggles were growing weaker. Somebody yelled and Hogue Kells rushed across to seize Traven by the shoulder.

'Let him up, you'll drown the—'

Traven lashed out and kicked Kells off his feet.

By this point everyone was shouting and men came running. Stang's half-submerged body had gone limp but Traven still showed no inclination to release the man, not even when Angelina appeared and screamed at him.

'Bastard was bad-naming Chett,' he panted, his eyes crazy. 'He won't do it again.'

'You'll kill him!' a cookhouse hand cried.

'So?'

Allison trotted across from the house with the colonel at his heels. He took the scene in at a glance, dashed to the trough and reefed at Traven's powerful arms.

'Leave go, Trav!'

But Traven either wouldn't or couldn't obey. In a blinding blur of motion, Allison swung a punch that hammered the side of Traven's face, breaking his stranglehold and driving him several feet along the side of the trough, where he staggered and fell.

It was several minutes before they had Stang properly revived, before a white-faced Allison turned to face a strangely subdued and still groggy Traven.

'That ties it, Trav,' he panted. 'We've got to be hard in this business, but we don't have to be loco.'

'I just can't believe you'd do such a thing, Mr Traven,' Angelina supported. 'And to think I was the foolish one who thought you weren't as wicked as others seemed to think.'

Shocked by the brutal incident, at witnessing Stang's near brush with death, the men gathered round, angry and suddenly emboldened by Allison's presence.

'The man's loco,' one accused. 'Colonel, you gotta get rid of him.'

Hannibal faced Traven but something in the gunman's eyes caused his mouth to run dry.

Next thing, Traven was gone.

In an instant he went plunging away into the surrounding darkness. Panting like a fox hunted by the hounds, he slumped against a wall of the barn with his burning face staring upwards, his mouth stretched like a knife wound.

He laughed aloud and the sound froze in his lungs like a cramp. He raised his hands to his face and pressed them harder and harder into his flesh, wrestling with the demons that had plagued him all his life and would hound him until he was dead.

# CHAPTER 9

# TOO PROUD TO DIE

It was a cold clear night with a high moon that threw the rangeland country into sharp relief, urging caution as heavily-armed bands of mounted men roamed across plateaux and benchlands.

There had been no contact with Cross-T in several days, but the scouts Allison had sent out during the day had warned of suspicious activity to the northwest.

From this, Allison deducted that the enemy might be plotting a strike against the Five-Mile bunkhouse, which stood in rough hill country where it commanded Five-Mile Valley. A large proportion of Hightower's main herd was grazing here.

This was deep in Hightower territory and Stobaugh hadn't dared venture this far in for quite a time. Still, with seven hands over-nighting at the bunkhouse, Chett reckoned he couldn't afford to take chances, and so led his group of riders for the valley at a swift lope.

Crossing the broad, low river flats, the party made good time until reaching the broken country that stretched all the way to the valley. They climbed a high mesa timbered with dwarf pine and great blue cedar bushes as shapely as Navajo jugs.

Traven noticed Chett staring back at the beautiful trees as they passed, and tugged his cigar from between his teeth.

'You know, pard, a man could get the notion that you ain't all that interested in this job of work tonight – that's if he didn't know you better.'

'That's a dumb thing to say.'

'Mebbe. But I still say it.'

'Free country.'

Traven scowled as they sloped down towards a narrow stream at the lope.

'Look, Chett, I told you I was sorry about what happened. What more can a man do?'

For a time it seemed Allison wouldn't answer. There'd been tension ever since the incident with Stang. Of course, this wasn't the first time two men of widely different style and temperaments had disagreed, but somehow this seemed more serious.

But finally Allison spoke. 'This is the last job, Trav.'

'What?'

'You heard.'

'The hell you say, man. Why, just on account I smashed a hick for bad-mouthing you—'

'It's not that.'

'What is it then? Angelina?'

'No.'

131

'Your beefing Stobaugh, then?'

Allison raised a long arm and pointed. 'There's the bunkhouse,' he said, and the conversation was over.

There was no trouble to be found in Five-Mile Valley. It was first light before they returned to head-quarters, and the matter the partners had touched on earlier wasn't mentioned again, then or later. But it wasn't forgotten.

Belden Harte wasn't at his office so Wolf Stobaugh went in search of him. The big man was in a hurry, something Buffalo Gate rarely saw from somebody who was so conscious of his size, power and dignity. But today the rancher wasn't himself, hadn't been ever since receiving the mysterious wire from down south, which at first he'd been tempted to screw up and throw away, until reminding himself he had a partner. He wanted Harte's opinion, then he would screw it up and throw it away.

But he didn't.

A short time later found him seated across from Harte in an alcove off the noisy barroom of the Indian Queen, intently studying the other's facial expressions as he scanned the message.

'So?' he demanded impatiently. 'What do you make of it?'

By way of reply, Harte held up the telegraph wire Wolf had received, then proceeded to read out loud:

'Stobaugh. I do not know you but I reckon you need me. I can help you in your troubles and will not charge you the world for reasons I can explain. Wire your reply to above address if interested. . . .'

Harte's voice faded as he looked up. 'Signed . . . Quint Nomad!'

'So?' Stobaugh's brow was corrugated. 'Everyone's heard of that gunner. But what's he want with us?'

'Isn't it obvious?' Harte's face was suddenly animated. The partnership had been enduring its rockiest period recently. Mostly doom and gloom. Not any longer. 'The man wants to join us – the cause. And for a fair price!'

'Why would he want to do that? I heard he charges like a bull for his services – or used to.'

'Let's find out, damnit!'

'You mean you're taking that thing serious? What if it's some kind of hoax? Nomad's one of the biggest names there are. He could charge whatever he likes to hire out. Why pick on us? Hell, man, I know we've been getting desperate, but I didn't know we were that far gone. Where are you going? I'm still talking, damn you.'

But Harte was already gone, the remains of his fifth brandy of the afternoon left standing on the table. The government man rarely touched the hard stuff but had done little but drink over the past week as he watched his dream slowly fading before his eyes, with finances nosediving critically while Hightower seemed to grow more ascendant with every passing day.

Wolf Stobaugh privately feared his partner was coming apart, yet at the same time sensed it to be far too late in the day to start thinking about dropping people, or changing horses midstream.

He strode through the staring barroom and lumbered out on to the porch.

He sighted Harte's bustling figure halfway down the block on the opposite side of Federation. The man was making for the telegraph office.

'Do you really believe Cross-T could be finally coming to understand it simply can't win this infernal feud, Chett?' The cattleman spoke hesitantly that quiet Sunday some days later. Hannibal appeared older, drawn. His banker had visited earlier and their financial position was looking grim. The cattleman was ready to clutch at straws.

'Well, they've tapered off despite what happened to Stobaugh's brother. . . .'

Allison glanced across the table at Angelina. She'd been a tower of strength since Casey Stobaugh's death. He needed that support. He cleared his throat and gazed out the window. 'I hear the fight is bleeding them even worse than us, so maybe there's hope. Of course, Stobaugh's never going to forget what happened, and I guess I don't blame him. But, in answer to your question, Colonel, yes, I'm dead sure they're weakening and I wouldn't be surprised if they called for a truce any day now.' He grimaced. 'A genuine truce, not like last time.'

'You cheered him up,' Angelina said later as the couple took coffee on the front gallery.

He half-smiled. 'Glad someone's cheerful.'

She was sober. 'You must forget it, Chett. It's over and done.'

'But maybe not finished.' He rose and gestured

towards the horse yards and stables.

'Want to take a look at the new foal?'

The afternoon passed slowly and pleasantly. Allison was mostly silent as they strolled, visited a couple of shot-up cowboys in the infirmary, wandered through the orchards in back of the house.

The girl was concerned for him, he realized. About his clash with Traven, the killing of Casey Stobaugh, his seeming withdrawal.

But there was no need, he knew. He was a man of the gun, and you learned early in the trade that regret could get you killed, that partnerships and friendships came and went. The reality of the situation was that he had already put both incidents behind him; the reason for his apparent moodiness was something quite different. Right now, Chett Allison was grappling with the question of his future. Of how he would survive once he'd hung up the guns – the biggest decision he'd had to make in over a decade, maybe in his entire life.

The evening was calm, there was an almost palpable air of confidence about the men as they came in off the range, a suggestion of swagger in working cowhands who had learned to become fighters, who'd grown accustomed to herding beef all day and riding their border with Cross-T by night.

Thre was no hint in this serene evening that sunset might be ushering in Hightower Ranch's most desperate night.

'Any sign, Bel?'

135

'Not yet.'

'Maybe he changed his mind and decided to come by stage?'

'His wire said he would get here sometime Wednesday – by horseback.'

'It's gone seven and starting to rain.'

'Do you think I don't know that—?'

Belden Harte bit off his words abruptly. Often in their partnership he found himself making most of the big decisions, considered himself the more intelligent, experienced and insightful of the pair. But he had to pull back at times and remind himself that Stobaugh was twice his size and very dangerous, which he was not. Even more significantly, Wolf owned fifteen thousand acres of grazing land and bossed a score of cowboys and gunhands while Belden J. Harte was still merely a minor governmental representative with big ideas, living in rented rooms on Kelly Street.

'I mean, Wolf, that perhaps I'm getting a bit edgy – this meeting being so important to me. Er, I mean to both of us, of course. You, me and the future.'

Stobaugh just scowled. He still wasn't overly impressed by the Nomad deal, still did not share Harte's excitement. He was plain and practical and just didn't believe some renowned gunman whose name used to be in all the papers a year ago, would suddenly bob up out of noplace and offer his services for a modest fee.

He'd rather go with the men he already had. Or more accurately, those he still had left. Cross-T hands were beginning to desert; the rot had set in after the kid was killed.

'Wolf!'

'What?'

'Look!'

The cattleman stared. The rider coming slowly along Federation rode a mean-looking Indian mustang with uncut mane and tail. He wore a grey Mackinaw and his hat was tilted against the thin rain.

But it had to be the gunfighter.

The way he carried himself and how his piercing eyes flicked this way and that, coupled with the shoulder-length white hair and tied-down guns – it could only be Quint Nomad.

It was.

A short time later the three were seated in the lobby of the Staghorn Hotel. The gunfighter had shed hat and coat and was the cynosure of all eyes as he sat straightbacked and alert in a sturdy wooden chair with a mug of coffee in hand, while his companions leaned forward on a leather divan clutching whiskies and hung on to his every word.

'I'll give it to you straight,' he stated, his voice strong and confident. 'I'm here to kill Allison.'

He held up a hand as they made to interject. They noticed how smooth and supple his every action was.

'Let me finish. I owe him and I'll pay him out. But when I learned he was tied up in this range war, I got to thinking it could work better if I was to sign up with you before choosing him out.'

'How come?'

Stobaugh couldn't conceal his eagerness now. Originally he had been lukewarm about Nomad's out-of-the-blue proposal. But meeting the fast gun had won him over. The man radiated a lethal assurance that was infectious.

'This isn't about money,' the gunman continued. 'I'd still have my day with Allison no matter what. But the way it is, if I just came out and braced him, alone, then what'd be to stop him coming after me with twenty guns? I'm not saying he would, but it could happen—'

'But if you sign with us, it would mean he'd have to play by the rules and either front you man to man, or run?' Harte anticipated eagerly.

'Correct.'

A well-dressed woman went by on the arm of a cattle-buyer from Duckwater. She gave the gunfighter a cool appraising stare. He gazed after her a moment but when he turned back they saw his brilliant eyes were like ice. This man had one thing on his mind in Buffalo Gate, and it wasn't women or money. He was a man with a mission.

'I'll be with you, with Cross-T,' he went on. He spread long-fingered hands. 'So he can fight me on my terms or be branded yellow. Either way he dies. Either way, you gents can't lose. What do you say?'

Harte and Stobaugh traded glances. From initial doubt, the rancher had now made the full transition to acceptance and excitement. Nomad was unique. His presence was almost hypnotic, and he had a way of making you believe his every brag. They were so impressed they already believed he could achieve what he predicted. Face Allison, bring him down, and as a consequence Hightower would lose its leadership and strength.

But Wolf Stobaugh had to be doubly sure. He wanted no lurking doubts undercutting him if they should take this step he proposed.

He said, 'Tell us about you and Allison.'

A flicker of annoyance crossed Nomad's deeply-tanned face. But then he shrugged, set his mug aside and took out the makings. As deft fingers shaped paper and tobacco into a neat white cylinder, he spoke as calmly as any diner reading the supper menu.

'Happened in the Goldmine country half a year ago, gents. I was heading up one bunch of no-accounts, Allison another. This night we came together by accident in a thunderstorm just outside a hell-hole named Pioche Butte. Well, to cut a long story short, wonderman Allison got lucky. He filled me with lead but somehow I managed to get away. I survived, but I went through hell, thinking about him every day . . . .'

Nomad's gaze was distant.

He was reliving the worst period of his life when even physical pain was secondary to the damage his pride had suffered. Then he shrugged wide shoulders, lighted up and flicked out the match.

'I came back from the Apache country planning to take up my trade where I left off. I knew I'd come to Allison sooner or later. But when I heard about your war . . .' He shrugged. 'Well, here I am.' His face turned hard, commanding. 'You want me to kill this wonder gun for you, or not?'

'Can . . . can you whip him?'

139

Stobaugh was sorry he spoke the moment the words were out.

'You sure you're a big man bossing a big range war?' Nomad asked sarcastically.

'Relax, er, Quint,' Harte said hastily. 'Wolf didn't mean anything. But you have to understand that we're just at about the end of our rope here. Another week and we might well go under . . . but let's not fret about that.'

He turned to Stobaugh. 'I guess we're both pretty impressed, right, Wolf?' The big man's nod was unhesitating. He was sold. 'Very well,' Harte went on. 'I can tell you now I've been boning up on you ever since we got your wire, and I couldn't be more impressed or confident. Very well, we'll guarantee you all the support you want if you go ahead and deal with Allison. Now, how will we go about it?'

'Just a minute,' Stobaugh cut in. 'Nomad, er . . . Quint, you do know about Traven, I guess?'

'The big man's shadow? Sure. What about him?'

'You brace Allison, you'll brace him, seems to me.'

Nomad shook his head. 'That's not the way we headliners operate, Stobaugh. Our reputations are worth more than yellow gold to us. We'll duel it out fair and square. After we've buried Allison we'll figure out what's to be done about his gun dog then. The man is fast but he's also a fool.'

He rose with sudden impatience.

'Enough talk. Is it a deal?'

Two heads nodded. It was unanimous.

Midnight, and the lights of Hightower headquarters

burned bright.

The messenger who'd brought the letter from town had now left. The stoves in house and cook-shack had been fired up again to boil coffee and fight off the chill of the rangeland for people who wouldn't be going back to their beds tonight.

The yard lamps were lighted and men wandered about clutching steaming pannikins. They spoke quietly amongst themselves and broke off frequently to gaze across at the house where flung shadows moved slowly to and fro across the drawn curtains.

Traven was scanning the letter yet again.

'. . . So there you have it, Allison. First light, Federation Street. Just you and me. If you don't show then I'll have to hunt you down like a yellow dog, and there's no telling how many other Hightower yellow dogs I might have to blow away to get to the hole you're hiding in. First light. Be there.'

The gunfighter looked up from the paper, eyes as black as pitch.

'This is likely phoney, Chett. We don't know Nomad's writing.'

'Nobody else ever called me a show pony.'

'But anyone might have written—'

'Forget it, Trav,' Allison cut in, standing tall behind Angelina's chair. 'It's him and we both know it. Who else would know I'd put exactly three bullets into him but him and me? And we didn't find him amongst the dead next day, remember?'

He nodded.

'It's Nomad, sure enough. And now he's linked up with Stobaugh and Harte,' he added with an air of

141

finality. 'The ace up their sleeve we didn't figure on. . . .'

'So, what do we do about it?' Hannibal seemed like a haggard old man. This war would kill him if it continued much longer.

'Do?' Allison appeared puzzled as he moved across to the mantle with his easy light step. 'There's only one thing to do, man.'

'Oh, Chett,' Angelina cried, jumping to her feet. 'You're not thinking of responding to this idiotic challenge, are you? You couldn't be.'

'You don't know this man, Angel,' he said quietly. 'He doesn't bluff, doesn't have to. If I don't meet him he won't just disappear. I damn near killed him. I wrecked his reputation. He's got to see it through.'

'There's a simpler way, pard.'

All stared at Traven, who was helping himself to the house's best brandy. He turned, glass in hand.

'I ride in tonight, look him up and give him six in the guts up close,' he grinned. 'Simple.'

'For pity's sake—' Angelina cried, but Allison cut her off.

'Obliged, Trav. But this is my deal. I didn't finish him back then, now it's time to complete the job.

He turned to the girl and took her hands.

'It's OK, Angel. He's good but not unbeatable. And there's a bright side. Nomad's the highest-priced gun in Nevada. Cross-T would have had to scrape the money barrel empty to meet his fee. That means that with Nomad out of the way they'll have to be ready to fold.' He glanced across at the cattleman. 'We'll win, and it will all be thanks to a gunman nobody is going to miss.'

It was some time before the gunfighters quit that big warm room, leaving behind the girl hysterical, her father bewildered, several house servants in tears.

The hands in the yard reacted to the news according to their temperament. Some paled at the notion of Allison fighting Nomad, others declared themselves ready and willing to saddle up and accompany him and Traven in to Buffalo Gate and deal with Nomad *en masse.*

They didn't realize Allison's decision was irrevocable.

Ned Traven did, however.

He was the only one who knew both Allison and Nomad, who'd fought with or against both men.

As a consequence the hardcase was alternately grinning contemptuously or frowning thoughtfully as everybody stood about in the freezing cold of the lantern-lit yard, talking the matter to death.

There was much Traven wanted to say to his partner, or could have said had he wanted to waste his breath. He knew Chett best. The moment he'd heard him declare he would face the killer, Traven knew the decision was final. The gate had slammed shut.

In a couple hours' time, Allison would saddle up and head for town to duel by the sacred code.

And die.

Whenever the chips were down and he had the time and interest to think a thing through, instead of blasting off half-cocked as he could do better than most anyone, Ned Traven could match wits with anybody.

His thinking had seldom seemed more crystal clear than now, which was the reason for the frown hiding behind his reckless, who-gives-a damn grin.

Ned Traven would boast to any man that Allison was the fastest and best. Yet in his savage heart he truly believed that should his friend face Quint Nomad on equal terms in Buffalo Gate, he would surely die.

# CHAPTER 10

# THE LAST NOTCH

Traven rode towards Buffalo Gate.

He rode steadily, neither fast nor slow and the darkness that was deepest just before dawn drew its mantle around him.

On either side of the trail great pines and gnarled and ancient cedars reared up, moaning and mourning in the wind. By daylight they were either blue or red-bowled, with silver-shimmering leaves under the wintry sun. Now they were dark and barely visible – giant witnesses to his passing.

The gunfighter felt very much alone with the cold air in his face and the night a dark shroud about him. Above the clop of the horse's hoofs, he could hear the faint burbling of the river as it trickled lazily across its pebbled bed. Occasionally he heard the stirring of a night bird or rodent in the brush.

145

It was a long time since he'd felt this good, if ever.

It seemed to him that the eternal conflicts of his life, its paradoxes and subtleties, the blacks and whites, had suddenly been resolved. It had been that way ever since riding clear of Hightower when he'd first grown aware of a strange cold current in his veins which warned him with certainty that death was waiting in the morning streets of the county capital.

He stirred in the saddle and glanced backtrail.

Back at the ranch, sprawled face-down in the straw in the darkness of the stables where he'd been readying his grulla for the journey to town, Chett lay unconscious with a long welt across his temple, put there by Traven's slashing gun barrel.

And as the gunmaster slept, his *segundo* wore his sober black broadcloth suit and flatbrimmed hat pulled low.

The tailored jacket was tight against his heavier shoulders but otherwise fitted well enough. He was timing his arrival in order that it would be light enough to duel by, but not so bright that onlookers might see more than they should.

He glanced down and thought; black – just the right colour for the business ahead. And asked himself with a twisted grin – could this be a genuine premonition of death he was experiencing as the slow horse miles passed behind him, or was he just dramatizing it all, as he was so often prone to do?

He'd scoffed at his 'death wish' in the past, attributing it to the melancholy that overcame him every so often. He'd lived most of his life with the stink of gunpowder about him, and the grisly spectre of death had breathed frostily in his face more times than he could recall. Each time he'd laughed at his own fears and had survived again and again.

But surely this feeling was different. Or could it be that he no longer wanted to survive?

He was readier to fight than he'd ever been, believed to the very core of his being that he could shade any gun living; Hickok, Harden – Nomad. He'd never been faster, had proven it every time he'd drawn his guns here. Why, he was even faster than Chett, though he'd die before he'd ever make that boast to any man.

The end of the partnership had been coming for a long time. He had known almost from the start that he'd deliberately played on Chett's sense of indebtedness to him to keep the thing going. It had been a lousy thing to do. But lousy was what he did best. Lousy, tricky, shifty, underhanded and selfish as a packrat. He was all those things and more. He'd always known it and his self-loathing might have brought him down long before this but for the fact that Allison had allowed him tag along, that at times he often felt they were genuine pards.

That had been vital to a man like himself, and his reasoning had been simple. If a man like Chett Allison was his friend, surely that proved that Ned Traven had some worth or value, impossible though it might be for others to recognize this fact.

He laughed aloud and the grulla pricked its ears.

All things must pass.

He hoped Chett would understand why he'd done

147

what he had, should this spooky feeling he had prove out and he didn't survive. Angelina too.

He smiled at thought of the girl and there was no self-mockery or cynicism in it. He'd like to be there when they married, if they ever got to be that sensible. But then, most likely he would offend somebody, start a fight, maybe even pinch a bridesmaid and get thrown out. Something, anything, you could always rely on Ned Traven to draw trouble like flies to a rib roast.

It was with a start of surprise that he realized that he was beginning to be able to make out the actual shapes of the trees on either side now.

Soon it would be day.

He knew that today the sun would rise as ever above the hills and mountains, climb over the wintry Nevadan plateau lands and rise to noon then fall, fade and finally disappear out there across the wide plains and deserts that led to California.

Just like always.

But would he see it?

One thing was for sure. He had it in his power to change this day. As ever, he made his own rules.

The timber fell away and he could see the town.

He lighted a stogie and it was good. By the time he flipped the stub away he was crossing the covered bridge leading into Chisum Street.

At first glance, Buffalo Gate appeared to be wrapped in sleep still, grey and sombre in the weak light with mist tatters drifting waist-high through hushed streets and and clinging to wet trees.

But the rider knew there would be people abroad.

Quint Nomad versus Chett Allison! That was surely a playbill guaranteed to drag even the most slothful citizen out of his warm blankets. And so what if there was a substitute for Allison. This substitute would not disappoint the customers. And in the weak dawn's light, and with black broadcloth coat and wide-crowned black hat, who could tell they weren't seeing the real thing?

He dismounted and tethered the grulla at the top end of Federation Street. Before him the street lay empty and silent. Then somebody coughed and somewhere along the street a window creaked open cautiously.

Slowly, with his long easy stride, the gunfighter began to walk.

By the time he'd covered half the block, it began to seep in that things were too quiet. That didn't figure, but it was something he might ponder on later. After it was over. The figure at the far end of Federation down by the Staghorn Hotel, was at first little more than a lighter patch against the greyness, but a dozen steps later and he defined the shape, another ten and he'd identified the man.

It was Nomad.

Now Traven felt the excitement begin to surge. Nomad made a stalwart, flamboyant figure standing there in the centre of the wide street. And what confidence any man must possess to be able to wait so calmly that way when confronting a man like Chett Allison! Allison had the reputation as invincible, and perhaps he was.

Only Traven – and maybe Chett himself for all he

149

knew – had the knowledge the former's hand was faster, his eye straighter. He knew Chett had experienced doubts about his survival in several gun duels in the past. Not his sidekick. Ned Traven always knew he would win. He had never met the man he didn't know he could kill.

He halted with a hundred feet between them. His adversary stepped a little to his right before halting again, touched hatbrim.

'You've beefed up some since Pioche Butte, Chett,' Nomad observed.

Traven didn't reply. His masquerade had proven effective thus far, but he would not risk speaking. Besides, there was nothing he had to say to a man prepared to go against his friend; a man he adjudged dead already.

He moved the broadcloth coat aside to reveal the double gunrig encircling his flat hips. The gesture was not wasted on Nomad. A feral grin worked the hawk face. He moved a little to present more of a profile target, his hand poised over his famed Colt.

'Any time, Chett.'

Traven stood as though carved from rock, only his shadowed eyes alive and agleam, boring at the fast gun's face. As the moments dragged by, he caught the first faint flicker of uncertainty in Nomad, then doubt, and finally anger.

'You're letting me make first move, Allison?' He sounded incredulous.

Still no response.

'Then die, hero. Burn in hell!'

Nomad's shout jarred the street end to end as his hand slashed downwards and the leaping bulk of his Colt whipped clear of leather, clean and precise.

'Trying to draw too fast,' Traven observed to himself as his own hand blurred and came up with a bucking Frontiersman .45 that belched yellow flame and roared out a stunning blast of sound that rocked the street.

Once, twice he fired, then holstered the smoking gun. His hand had come clear of the weapon before Nomad's knees buckled and he fell forward to strike the street with his face.

Slowly Traven stepped back and turned his head to sweep falsefronts, alleyways and darkened windows and doorways, a faint perplexity stirring his features.

The gunshots would have awakened the dead, yet still no sign of life.

'Show yourselves, you Stobaugh toads! You too, Harte. Come out and see the man you just got killed. Your big play blew up in your faces, and you're gonna see it and admit it. Get out here before I come in after you, yeller-bellies!'

This drew an astonished gasp from the darkened saloon, and a voice that could have been Wolf Stobaugh's was heard to choke out, 'Great Judas! That ain't Allison – it's Traven!'

Traven's laugh was a throaty roar as he whipped out his gun again and the big plate glass front window of the hotel went out with a crash as he squeezed trigger.

'Come on you milk-sucking whore-dogs—' he began, but a louder almost hysterical voice drowned him out.

'Get him!'

Harte's voice. At the command a dozen menacing shapes abruptly filled alley-mouths and loomed up from behind falsefronts, menacing silhouettes with sixguns and rifles gleaming in their hands.

'The bastards!' Traven growled, almost admiringly. 'Why didn't I figure they wouldn't play it straight. . . ?'

He laughed at the top of his lungs and brought a man crashing down from atop the Feed and Grain barn with a .45 bullet through the heart.

Instantly the street trembled to the drumroll of guns that mounted to a roar, and the towering figure in the centre of the street reeled and staggered with death filling the air, bullet-whipped dust spuming all about him.

Traven was hit and hit again. Yet the wild laughter continued as he staggered, straightened, brought another man down – and another.

Then he was reeling backwards and the ugly sound of lead striking flesh punctuated the roaring volley, and Traven turned his face to the empty skies.

So this was what it was like – he'd often wondered. He craved, with fierce desperation, to raise his guns just one last time and take another with him. But his sixgun weighed a ton and his arm was weak as a girl's. He grunted softly as another bullet struck home, the singing of the guns sounding high and distant. Somehow he turned and looked east. The sun was just lifting clear of the hills as he fell.

*

They didn't hear the horses. They were still deafened by the gunfire that had continued insanely for a full half-minute after Traven fell, the force of the volleys causing his body to twitch and roll as though still alive.

Clutching smoking guns and still eyeing the riddled giant warily, even though knowing he was dead, Wolf Stobaugh and his gunmen rushed into the street with wondering faces. In the space of a minute they'd witnessed a duel they would never forget, followed by the spectacle of a man defying death far more fiercely than anyone would have thought possible.

Then a gun roared and a bullet whipped the length of Federation Street to smack hard and flat into the front wall of the bank, powdering brick.

As one they whirled to see them – Chett Allison riding at the head of a dozen Hightower riders as they swung round the emporium corner, bristling with guns, faces pale and raging in the new light as they spread to fill the street from one side to the other and stormed forward, a wall of steel and terror.

The Cross-T ambushers had been too eager to rush to the centre of the street to view Ned Traven at close quarters, to reassure themselves the man was truly dead.

Now suddenly they were terribly exposed, and an ashen Wolf Stobaugh lifted his hands high and began shouting at the oncoming horsemen, desperate to explain, to lie, maybe to buy enough time to make cover.

Too late.

Allison, who'd rounded the corner well ahead of the main force, had seen Traven go down, had heard the ugly roar of triumph from the ambushers as they rushed from concealment. That was all he needed to see, and now his twin sixguns stormed with fierce authority and his flanking guns chimed in, tearing the morning apart, drowning out the cries and curses of men trying to outrun death.

Drum Cormorant, not the best but perhaps the bravest of the Cross-T fighting force, alone chose to stand his ground. Dropping into a low crouch behind Quint Nomad's sprawled figure, he emptied a saddle and was lining up on another rider when he was hit. He spun, triggered repeatedly into the dirt then crashed down as a fierce volley scythed him off his feet.

Cormorant's defiance was the single display of real courage in the face of odds. But although bewildered and scattered by the ferocity of the Hightower attack, there were skilled guns and desperate ones amongst the men who went diving for cover, looking for a run-out or returning fire as the rolling guns rushed ever closer.

Hightower men tumbled and more would surely have joined them but for Allison. He'd seen Traven's riddled corpse, and it was as though he had no fear as he slowed before the saloon to blast one running figure after another off their feet with sixguns that seemed incapable of missing their targets.

Inspired, the Hightower force fanned wide and broke up to go spurring down side streets and alleys in pursuit of survivors. Screams rose ragged and shrill, and someone with blood spilling from his mouth cried out to God to spare him in a voice that seemed to reach every corner of town before a hard-riding Hogue Kells's big hunting rifle blasted him into eternity, ready or not.

Wolf Stobaugh made the front porch of the Staghorn before going down with a shattered leg. Raging with disbelief at the way victory was dissolving before his eyes, he emptied one saddle and was lining up Buck Taller when two riders homed in on him. This was Stobaugh's war and he left it without a whimper as the riders got his range and didn't miss.

A fleeing Belden Harte, heart thudding and wild-eyed with fear, almost got clear before a cowboy on a pale horse came from a side alley and raised his gun to fire before realizing who he had in his sights. He was just a simple cowhand turned gunman, but showed himself smart enough to realize firstly that Harte was unarmed, and secondly that if any man might supply all the answers people were going to need about this evil night, it had to be him – so ran him down and took him prisoner. Allison was dismounting in the centre of a suddenly quiet main street as the rider returned with his prisoner on the end of a lasso. Everywhere, men were getting off excited horses, examining wounds, tallying the dead and wounded.

The battle was over, the final battle of the Vulcan County War.

Doors opened hesitantly all along the stem, most just a little at first but were then flung wide when it was realized it was truly over; someone cheered hoarsely, somewhere a woman began to weep.

Colonel Hannibal and his driver were standing by the ranch surrey near Traven's body as Allison approached.

'Get away from him,' he snapped as Hannibal bent over the dead man.

'He's dead, Chett,' the cattleman said in a half whisper.

Traven's face, caked with mud, was grinning still. Blood spread wide.

Allison bent and hefted the heavy body. He carried it the short distance to the Buckhorn and mounted the steps. His bootheels sounded loudly on the planking as he walked to the doors. He backed through the batwings, gently angling Traven's muddied head past the doors.

Inside, grunting a little now with his burden, he moved with heavy steps towards the faro layout. He laid Traven on the table amongst chips and counters and silver pieces, where the all-night game had halted. He straightened the dead man's legs then took a silk kerchief from his pocket and placed it gently over the face.

Peering through windows and over the tops of the batwings, citizens and and ranch hands made to enter.

'Get out!'

Allison's voice sent them scuttling for cover.

Then he walked across to the bar. He took down a

glass and a bottle of Green River and poured himself a whiskey. He raised it and nodded to the still figure on the table. 'How, Trav.'

Traven's funeral was postponed until after the initial two-day hearing conducted by the county judge from the capital, during which Belden Harte had cracked and confessed under the prosecution's attack and was now on his way to the capital to face trial. Most of Buffalo Gate watched them bury Ned Traven, now virtually the entire town watched as Allison rode out. He looked much as he had done the first day he'd ridden down the main street, preceded by a legend. He still wore black broadcloth and white linen shirt, and his flat black hat was at the same accurate angle they'd grown familiar with. He looked a little pale, but they were accustomed to that as they were to other things about him that made him seem different from most men – the ugly and odd-coloured horse, the guns, the aura of a man and a gunfighter.

They were saddened to see him go, were puzzled that the colonel's daughter, watching from the court-house gallery, alone in that crowd seemed cheerful, even happy.

But this was no mystery. For she alone in all that throng knew that when the dust had cleared and Vulcan County had settled into the good life he'd done so much to help achieve, he would be coming back. To her.